"You're saying we wouldn't have a real marriage?"

"For legal purposes we would."

"And what would that do to Flynn and Jason? They'll get to know you, love you, think of you as their mother. Then you'd up and leave. What would that do to them?"

What would her leaving do to him? Cameron thought.

"And if my grandparents win custody, how much will it hurt the boys to lose their father?" Alexa countered.

"What about your work?"

"I'll put it on hold."

Cameron didn't want to ask her to make this sacrifice. But he couldn't lose his boys.

Images of Alexa protecting the twins from yesterday's danger gnawed at him. She was brave and vibrant and full of life and if he tried to keep her here permanently, would she wither and blame him?

Alexa took his hand between hers. "I couldn't live with myself if I let you down. So call your father. Tell him we're having a wedding."

Dear Harlequin Intrigue Reader,

The days are getting cooler, but the romantic suspense is always hot at Harlequin Intrigue! Check out this month's selections.

TEXAS CONFIDENTIAL continues with *The Specialist* (#589) by Dani Sinclair. Rafe Alvarez was the resident playboy agent, until he met his match in Kendra Kincaide. He transformed his new partner into a femme fatale for the sake of a mission, and instantly lost his bachelor's heart for the sake of love....

THE SUTTON BABIES have grown in number by two in *Little Boys Blue* (#590) by Susan Kearney. A custody battle over cowboy M.D. Cameron Sutton's baby boys was brewing. When East Coast socialite Alexa Whitfield agreed to a marriage of convenience, Cam thought his future was settled. Until he fell for his temporary wife— the same wife someone was determined to kill!

Hailed by *Romantic Times Magazine* as an author who writes a "tantalizing read," Gayle Wilson returns with *Midnight Remembered* (#591), which marks the conclusion of her MORE MEN OF MYSTERY series. When ex-CIA agent Joshua Stone couldn't remember his true identity, he became an easy target. But his ex-partner Paige Daniels knew all his secrets, including what was in his heart....

Reeve Snyder had rescued Polly Black from death and delivered her baby girl one fateful night. Polly's vulnerable beauty touched him deep inside, but who was she? And what was she running from? And next time, would Reeve be able to save her and her daughter when danger came calling? Find out in *Alias Mommy* (#592) by Linda O. Johnston.

Don't miss a single exciting moment!

Sincerely,

Denise O'Sullivan
Associate Senior Editor
Harlequin Intrigue

LITTLE BOYS BLUE
SUSAN KEARNEY

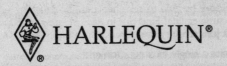

HARLEQUIN®

TORONTO • NEW YORK • LONDON
AMSTERDAM • PARIS • SYDNEY • HAMBURG
STOCKHOLM • ATHENS • TOKYO • MILAN • MADRID
PRAGUE • WARSAW • BUDAPEST • AUCKLAND

ISBN 0-373-22590-3

LITTLE BOYS BLUE

Copyright © 2000 by Susan Hope Kearney

This edition published by arrangement with Harlequin Books S.A.

® and TM are trademarks of the publisher. Trademarks indicated with
® are registered in the United States Patent and Trademark Office, the
Canadian Trade Marks Office and in other countries.

Visit us at www.eHarlequin.com

Printed in U.S.A.

ABOUT THE AUTHOR

Susan Kearney used to set herself on fire four times a day. Now she does something really hot—she writes romantic suspense. While she no longer performs her signature fire dive, she never runs out of ideas for characters and plots. A business graduate from the University of Michigan, Susan has written eleven novels and writes full-time. She resides in a small town outside Tampa, Florida, with her husband and children and a spoiled Boston terrier. She's currently plotting her way through her next novel.

Books by Susan Kearney

HARLEQUIN INTRIGUE

340—TARA'S CHILD
378—A BABY TO LOVE
410—LULLABY DECEPTION
428—SWEET DECEPTION
456—DECEIVING DADDY
478—PRIORITY MALE
552—A NIGHT WITHOUT END
586—CRADLE WILL ROCK*
590—LITTLE BOYS BLUE*

*The Sutton Babies

THE SUTTONS

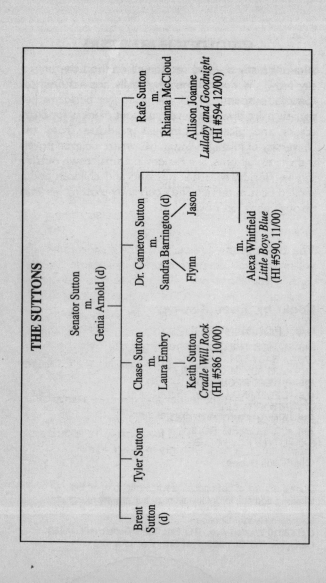

Senator Sutton
m.
Genia Arnold (d)

Brent Sutton (d)

Tyler Sutton

Chase Sutton
m.
Laura Embry

Keith Sutton
Cradle Will Rock
(HI #586 10/00)

Dr. Cameron Sutton
m.
Sandra Barrington (d)

Flynn   Jason

m.
Alexa Whitfield
Little Boys Blue
(HI #590, 11/00)

Rafe Sutton
m.
Rhianna McCloud

Allison Joanne
Lullaby and Goodnight
(HI #594 12/00)

CAST OF CHARACTERS

Alexa Whitfield—She has the perfect job, the perfect life. But when tragedy strikes, she has hard choices to make.

Dr. Cameron Sutton—He kisses like an angel, makes love like the devil. And he's set on turning Alexa's perfect world upside down.

Jason and Flynn Sutton—Twin two-year-olds who make trouble as easily as they do mud pies. They will grow up to inherit one of the richest estates in America. And that potential wealth makes them a target.

The Barringtons—Alexa's wealthy grandparents are willing to take Cameron to court to contest custody of their grandsons. But will they resort to murder and kidnapping to get control of the boys' trust fund?

Julie Edwards—The college coed and the twins' baby-sitter has three attractive men ready to court her, but the man she wants is out of reach.

Cody Barnes—The shy young man is always around when there's trouble.

Leo Harvey—Bodybuilder and cook; he wants Julie, but how far will he go to get her?

Bodine Stone—The head foreman; is he an honest employee or a man with his own agenda?

For Debbie and Russ, Keith and Craig.

Prologue

"Don't be silly, Alexa," her cousin Sandra Sutton lectured. "You can watch the twins for the five minutes it'll take me to fetch us hot dogs and coffee."

Seeking to halt a rising sense of unease, Alexa Whitfield risked insulting her cousin by attempting to refuse. "I don't—"

"—know anything about babies," Sandra finished for her, an indication of how many times Alexa had used that particular excuse to avoid holding and feeding Flynn and Jason over the past few days of her visit.

Determined not to show her trepidation, Alexa neatly folded the *Boston News* and set the paper beside her on the park bench with a forced smile. "*I'll* get coffee."

"For Pete's sake. The twins are sleeping." Sandra stood, handed her the diaper bag filled with baby paraphernalia, beating Alexa to a clean getaway. Sandra's fashionable heels clicked along the pavement, but after a few steps, she turned back with a smile of encouragement. "You'll never learn to enjoy kids if you aren't willing to try."

"By the time you get back, I'll be an expert." Despite her inner turmoil, Alexa made her voice sound lighthearted.

"Just don't drop them," Sandra instructed as she fluffed her auburn hair with her hand.

"As if I didn't know that," Alexa grumbled.

Alexa Whitfield could identify a genuine Picasso from a fake at twenty paces, but if Flynn or Jason so much as burped, she wouldn't know what to do. Not that she didn't think the twins were adorable. She did. Not that she didn't want to scoop them up and bury her nose in their baby-soft skin. She'd love to.

Fate had decreed, however, that Alexa could never be a mommy. Some women couldn't stay on a diet, others didn't have the discipline to exercise regularly, some suffered from insomnia. Alexa couldn't bear children, but she didn't dwell on her inability. Not when life had so much else to offer.

While Sandra had the love of her adoring husband, Dr. Cameron Sutton, and the twins; Alexa had a passion for her work and a life most women would envy. Purchasing museum-quality art sent Alexa to Rio during Carnivale, Paris in the spring and New York City in the fall. She'd been invited to the White House for dinner, attended parties in Milan, London and Rome. European royalty often sought her advice.

Alexa stared at the Sutton twins asleep in their strollers and wished she had her sketch pad. She'd love to capture the babies' round cheeks, the dimples, the black hair they'd inherited from their brilliant father and the contrasting fair skin from their mother.

Leaning down, Alexa tucked in the blanket by Flynn's feet, smoothed back Jason's hair, surprised by the satisfaction the tiny gesture gave her.

A shrill scream brought Alexa's head snapping up from the stroller.

Sandra!

Dear God, the scream had sounded like her cousin. As people ran down the path Sandra had taken, Alexa's fear shifted into high gear. Since the plane crash that had taken both sets of parents when they were youngsters, the cousins had been raised together by their wealthy Barrington grandparents, and Alexa loved Sandra like a sister.

Don't panic. Sandra would come walking around the bend any minute, juggling hot dogs and coffee, tossing her auburn hair back from her eyes, ready to tell Alexa what the excitement was all about.

Two minutes later a siren wailed and Flynn awakened—at least she thought it was Flynn. Alexa was still having trouble telling the boys apart. With wide, frightened eyes, he looked for his mother, and when he couldn't find her, he started to cry until huge tears rolled down his chubby cheeks.

Awkwardly but without hesitation, Alexa picked him up. But not before Jason awoke and also started to howl.

"Now what? I don't have four arms." At her words the babies' cries subsided and she returned Flynn to the stroller. If she hadn't been so worried about Sandra, she would have been pleased by how easily she'd comforted the boys.

"Where's your mother?" Alexa checked her watch. Sandra had been gone more than ten minutes.

Should she stay and wait? If Sandra returned to find Alexa and her babies gone, would she worry?

Alexa decided to walk the stroller up the block to the corner hot-dog stand and come straight back. Most likely she'd run into Sandra, who'd probably stopped to chat with an acquaintance.

Shoving the baby stroller into motion, she walked briskly down the sidewalk, determined to give Sandra a piece of her mind for scaring her so. Palms sweaty, Alexa rounded the corner to see yellow police tape cordoning off a crime scene.

Heart pounding, fear hastening her footsteps, Alexa hurried until her pace behind the baby stroller almost reached a jog. Shoving her way through the crowd, she took one look at the victim's cap of auburn hair and her knees turned to jelly.

"Sandra!"

A cop noticed Alexa and jerked his thumb toward the pavement where her cousin was being loaded onto a stretcher. "You know this woman?"

"My cousin." Alexa swallowed hard at the huge amount of blood on the sidewalk.

"She was mugged with a baseball bat." The kindly cop took Alexa's arm. "They're taking her to Boston Memorial but…"

At the implication that Sandra might not survive long enough to reach the hospital, tears brimmed in Alexa's eyes. "Can I see her?"

A minute later Alexa was leaning over her cousin as the paramedics strapped in her cousin. "Sandra?"

At the sound of Alexa's voice, Sandra turned her head, her beautiful clear blue eyes clouded with pain. "Tell Cam I love him."

"You can tell him yourself. I'll call him and he'll be waiting at the hospital."

Sandra convulsed, her entire body shuddering, but she kept talking. "Promise me."

"Anything."

"My boys. Take care of them."

"You'll get better. *You'll* take care of them."

Sandra grabbed her hand with waning strength. "Don't let...the grandparents...raise them."

"Hang on, Sandra. Fight. You and Cameron will raise the boys."

"No boarding schools. No nannies."

"They have their mother," Alexa insisted.

Sandra grasped Alexa's hand, refusing to let the paramedics put her in an ambulance until she had an answer. "Promise me."

Tears clogged Alexa's throat. "I promise."

Chapter One

Highview, Colorado
One year later

The telephone rang and Dr. Cameron Sutton hesitated, his hand over the receiver like a wary medical student entering the operating room for the first time. Cam had been notified of his deceased wife's mugging by telephone. Told of the upcoming custody battle with Sandra's grandparents over the twins by telephone. And ever since *Humanity Today* had named him Boston's most eligible bachelor, it seemed as if every damn reporter in the country felt they had the right to invade his privacy.

Escaping from Boston to the Sutton ranch in Highview, Colorado, had kept intruders at a physical distance. Caller ID would have helped maintain his privacy, but suppose a patient needed him? Too responsible to ignore the possible need of someone sick or injured, Cam picked up the phone. "Yes?"

"It's Alexa."

Recognizing the cultured voice of his wife's cousin, Cam relaxed in his padded leather rocker.

Propping his feet on his desk, he looked out his window and let the brilliant Colorado sunshine and verdant mountains that surrounded the vast Sutton acreage of his boyhood home calm his apprehension.

"I'm calling from the airport."

Hong Kong? Budapest? Marakesh? Cam didn't ask or bother to keep up with Alexa's hectic schedule. While he commended Sandra's cousin for her monthly calls to check on the twins, he couldn't keep back a niggle of suspicion about her timing. Only yesterday, his attorney had notified him that Sandra and Alexa's grandparents had filed for custody of his boys. Despite the Barringtons' wealth, Cam wasn't too worried—not with his father, a Colorado senator, in his corner.

"The twins love it out here," he told Alexa before she could ask. On the Sutton cattle ranch, his twin prodigies could grow up with more freedom from scrutiny than in the city. "The Senator gave each of them a pony last week."

Alexa gasped. "They're only two years old!"

Cam chuckled and started to tease her, then recalled how little Alexa knew about children. And how a sharp attorney might use the ponies in court during a custody battle. Cam didn't want to give even the appearance of recklessness and did his best to keep the defensiveness from his voice. "My nephew, Keith, has been riding almost since he could walk."

"Still—"

"We never let the boys near the horses without supervision. And you know Julie grew up out here and around horses."

Alexa sighed. "Julie is a wonderful baby-sitter. You're lucky to have her."

"Yes, we are." Cam had been grateful when Julie had agreed to move back to Colorado with him and the boys. Julie Edwards had come to work for their family after Judge Stewart, an associate of his father's, had recommended her. Although she'd grown up in Colorado, she'd agreed to move to Boston after the twins were born. And Cam was grateful she'd agreed to move back out west after Sandra's death. The adaptable nanny had eased the twins through the loss of their mother with surprising compassion for a college sophomore.

"Is Julie working today?"

"She's leaving any minute for class. Why?"

"I was hoping she could give me a lift. This airport doesn't have cab service." Cam frowned in confusion.

Alexa laughed. "I suppose I should have phoned ahead, but I wanted to surprise you."

She certainly had. Alexa, normally so clear and logical, wasn't making any sense. "You flew into Highview?"

"Straight from Rome, via New York and Denver."

What the hell? Cam scratched his head and looked around his barely framed-in home, which was still under construction and not the least bit ready for a guest—especially one accustomed to the Ritz-Carlton in Paris, Claridge's in London and the Plaza in New York City. Plumbers had yet to hook up the final water line from the well. Carpenters hadn't finished the staircase banister to the second story, and there was still a mammoth-size gap in his office window frame waiting for an oversize pane of glass to arrive. Surprisingly the swimming-pool contractor had almost finished.

From his silence, Alexa must have sensed his hesitation. "Can we discuss my visit in person? I'm afraid I didn't change enough lira into quarters."

Just as she finished her sentence, the phone went silent, then the dial tone pealed accusingly in his ear. During Alexa's infrequent but regular phone calls, she'd mentioned she might visit the twins, and he'd issued a blanket invitation, but Cam had never expected her to take him up on the offer. Not without warning. Certainly not while his house was still under construction.

With swift precision, he stood and checked his watch. When his baby-sitter had agreed to return to Highview with his family, he'd promised her he would schedule around her classes at the local college. She lived at the dorm and took classes in the afternoons and the occasional evening. If he brought the twins with him to the airport, he wouldn't have to ask Julie to miss her afternoon class.

And once Alexa saw his sons' capacity for finding trouble, Cam figured he wouldn't have to try very hard to convince her to stay at the Highview Hotel.

A year of handling the precocious twins without Sandra's help had made Cam nothing if not efficient. Within ten minutes he'd said goodbye to Julie and strapped Flynn and Jason into the toddler seats of his sport-utility vehicle, gathering toys and snacks along the way.

Flynn hated to sit still for more than ten seconds,

especially when there was a yard filled with mud, interesting pipes, ditch-digging equipment and fencing to explore. He kicked his feet and pointed out the window. "Juk."

"Junnnk," Cam automatically corrected his eldest by four minutes, emphasizing the *N* sound, not in the least surprised the two-year-old remembered Cam calling the rusty equipment junk.

"Not junk." Jason disagreed. "Play toys."

"You're an optimist, junior." Cam shook his head at the younger twin, reminding himself of the need to be ever vigilant. A construction site was no place for curious toddlers. Nor was the Senator's mansion with its too many breakables. His twins didn't have the judgment to go with their incomparable intelligence.

Cam's respect for the Senator, who had raised five sons out here after their mother died, went up another notch. Although he and his brothers had been hellions, they'd turned into mostly respectable citizens. And he hoped to instill the same values in his kids that his father had in him—a love of the land, a confidence in oneself and a loyalty to family.

The Sutton acreage was a working cattle ranch that the Senator had recently bequeathed to Cam and his three brothers. His brothers had watched over his portion, but after Sandra's death, Cam had returned to Highview to build a home, staking claim to forty acres and intent on starting a medical practice in town. So far he'd managed to do neither. But he had no doubt that eventually he would settle in comfortably here, and the boys seemed to thrive in the open air, spoiled by their uncles and grandfather.

After leaving home at eighteen, Cam had always intended to return to Colorado. But when he went East for college and then medical school, attaining the best education money could buy, he'd fallen in love with Sandra Barrington, great-granddaughter of Arthur Levenger, nineteenth-century robber baron and industrialist, and the granddaughter of Boston's high-society Barringtons had captured his heart. Sandra wouldn't consider leaving Boston and the grandparents who'd raised her and her cousin, Alexa. So Cam had set up a practice back East and tried to appreciate the wealthy clientele the Barrington connections threw his way.

After Sandra's murder, Cam had craved the isolation of the ranch and the comforting acceptance of family and friends. Out here, a man had room to breathe. And grieve. Sandra's senseless death still clawed at him, but not only because her murder had never been solved. In a big-city park filled with lovers, joggers and vendors, no one had seen anything. As the months passed without a lead, Cam had given up on the police ever catching her murderer, but he hadn't given up wishing that Sandra could be here to share the twins with him.

He ached to turn to her and brag about their sons' uncommon intelligence, their sheer exuberance for life. She would never see her sons grow to maturity. Never see them take their first steps, hear their first words. Not only did Cam miss Sandra for himself, it pained him that the boys would have no memory of their mother.

Cam had once asked the Senator how he'd managed to go on after his own wife, Cam's mother, had died, leaving his father to raise five sons. The Senator had squeezed his shoulder and told him that while his wife was gone forever, his memories of her would never die. At that moment some of Cam's pain had eased. The boys might not remember Sandra, but he could tell them stories about her. He still missed his wife and always would, but like his father, he had found the strength to go on. Luckily the twins kept him busy enough that he didn't have time to brood.

Even now as he pulled onto the private Sutton road that led to town, he caught sight of Jason fiddling with the strap that kept him buckled into the toddler seat. Another thirty seconds and he'd work himself free.

From experience Cam knew that the best way to control the twins was by distraction. If he could engage their curious minds, their busy fingers might stop probing, twisting and turning every button, knob, dial and switch within reach.

He tossed a spherical plastic puzzle into the back seat. "Here, you two. See if you can take that puzzle apart."

With surprisingly accurate reflexes that reminded Cam of his younger brother Rafe, Flynn caught the plastic ball between two chubby hands. "Mine."

"Share," Jason insisted.

Cam smiled at the success of his ploy, turned past the barn and swung onto pavement just as the plumbing truck rounded the bend, heading toward his muddy driveway. Cam slowed and rolled down his window, glancing at the unclouded blue sky and the July sun directly overhead, then at the plumbers.

''You guys were supposed to be here first thing this morning.''

''Sorry, Dr. Sutton. We were waiting on a culvert. You said you wanted the water lines hooked up to the house today.''

''Yeah, I'd like to try bathing the boys in a bathtub instead of a horse trough.''

Flynn tossed the ball to his brother. ''No bath.''

''Like dirt,'' Jason agreed.

''Pipe down in the chorus,'' Cam ordered.

''What's a chorus?'' Flynn asked.

''Us.'' Jason found the key and pulled out the first puzzle piece.

Cam rolled up his window and wondered if the two boys were reverting to little savages. They liked to crawl and dig in the mud. They preferred to pee outside, and without indoor plumbing, what could he expect?

Perhaps he should have kept the boys at the Senator's house until his house was complete. But Cam was reluctant to leave the boys with anyone but Julie. In the last year, the boys had been through so much, losing their mother and moving from Boston to Colorado had changed all their lives. He didn't want the twins to feel as if they'd lost their father, too. And since Cam needed to oversee the construction, he'd kept the boys at his side.

He glanced over his shoulder at the twins and reassured himself the boys were still buckled in and reasonably clean. Julie had washed their hair this morning, and if they looked in need of haircuts, at least they smelled of baby shampoo. With their heads

so close together they almost bumped, the two boys
were firmly engrossed in the puzzle.

As he headed to Highview's private airport, he recalled that the last time Alexa had seen the boys,
they'd just learned to crawl. Sandra had mentioned
her cousin had been reluctant to hold the babies even
while she'd been captivated by them. Now they were
little bundles of restless energy. What would Alexa
think of them?

"I BROUGHT PRESENTS," Alexa said through smiling
apple-red lips as she scooped a squirming Flynn into
her arms at the airport with the ease of someone accustomed to wriggling toddlers.

Cam hadn't seen her since her tragic visit to Boston last year, but he noted her new ease with the
children and was fascinated by it. Her eyes sparkled
with excitement as she held Flynn with a competence
he'd never expected.

"Candy?" Flynn stopped wriggling long enough
for Alexa to plant a kiss on his forehead and ruffle
his hair.

Resting on Cam's hip, Jason's ears perked up.
"Gum?"

"What did I tell you boys about begging?" Cam
tried to keep the laughter out of his voice.

Alexa might not have known much about kids a
year ago, but she'd learned fast, and he wondered if,
in the intervening months, she'd met a man with children. She hadn't mentioned a personal relationship
during her phone calls, but Alexa tended to be a private person. However, she'd already won the twins
over by mentioning presents.

Cam was glad that his sons had Alexa's attention. He didn't remember her ever looking so vibrant. Highview's airport, only for small private planes, didn't boast a terminal, and Alexa shined on the tarmac like a ruby amid dark gravel. Her cherry-red suit and matching spiked heels set off her blunt-cut, shoulder-length dark hair to perfection. Flawlessly groomed, freshly powdered and glossy-lipped, Alexa could fly for twenty-four hours straight and disembark from a plane looking ready for a model's runway.

Yet she'd come ready to do battle and win over the twins. With a vivacious face that exuded a lively intelligence, Alexa opened a red patent-leather purse, rooted around and retrieved two Chinese paper puzzles.

"Here." She handed one to each boy without a word of explanation.

"Tell Alexa thank you," Cam reminded his sons.

"Lexi, thanks."

"Me, too."

"You're welcome," Alexa told them.

Cam watched Alexa's eyes light with anticipation as she waited for his sons to stick their fingers in each end of the puzzle, saw her restrain a smile as the paper puzzle trapped their fingers.

"Sticky."

"Very sticky."

"Stuck," Cam said, his correction lost in the roar of a plane taxiing for takeoff.   •

Alexa swiveled Flynn onto her hip, swung her purse strap over her other shoulder to free one hand. "Push."

Carrying the always wriggling twins was never easy, but Alexa accomplished the maneuver like a professional nanny who was enjoying her task. Either she'd been baby-sitting a lot or she'd taken up juggling.

Eyes bright with amusement, Alexa guided his son's hands. As Flynn's fingertips moved together, the puzzle released his fingers. "Kew-el."

In moments Jason, too, had freed his hands and then immediately stuck his fingers back into the trap. "Do it again."

Cam steered Alexa and the boys over to the baggage area where the pilot unloaded luggage from the small plane. "Where's your bag?"

Alexa tilted her head toward a cart of elegant black leather luggage with gold designer braid. Cam headed for the baggage, doing his best to conceal his surprise and dismay at the number of suitcases. He counted six, as well as a garment bag, a heavy-duty trunk and a computer case, and wondered exactly how long Alexa planned to stay.

Cam stowed the last suitcase into the SUV while Alexa strapped the boys into their seats. "How about lunch in town at—"

"Big Mac?" Jason asked.

"Yes. Yes. Yes!" Flynn echoed his brother's request to visit the golden arches.

Cam shot an apologetic look at Alexa. "I was thinking of lunch at the Highview Hotel." Where afterward he could leave her in a room with hot and cold running water, heat or air-conditioning and room service.

Alexa took one look at the boys' expressions and turned back to Cam. "I'd love a hamburger."

"Lexi rules." The two boys high-fived each other, a favorite gesture that Rafe had taught them while he gave them riding lessons on the ponies. As Cam stole a look at Alexa, he drove into town, grateful for the boys' exuberance and chatter. He couldn't help wondering about the reasons for Alexa's unexpected visit or how long she intended to stay, but realized it wouldn't be polite to ask.

Alexa crossed one smoothly stockinged leg over the other, distracting Cam as her skirt inched up her thigh. It must be the high-spiked red heels that made her legs look so long—or he certainly would have noticed them before now. Alexa had danced at his engagement party—been maid of honor at his wedding—wearing a stunning silver gown, and he'd seen her in somber black at Sandra's funeral. But he'd never noticed her spectacular legs before.

Once Sandra had come into his life, Cam had stopped looking at other women—at least in a sexual way. He'd loved his wife, and since her death, he'd seemed to have lost all interest in the sweeter sex. But Alexa's legs were waking him up, as if from a long, drowsy sleep, and he shifted uncomfortably.

Although he was pleased that the grief was finally lifting from his heart, Alexa was Sandra's cousin, and he felt disloyal to Sandra for even looking at another woman. Especially Alexa. His wife and Alexa were cousins, losing both their parents, who'd been on a ski vacation together, in the same plane crash. Cameron knew his wife and Alexa were more like sisters than cousins, and he'd always thought of Alexa in the same way. To think of her as a woman was disconcerting.

Besides, Alexa was merely visiting. She was passionate about her career, switching time zones and continents the way other women switched underwear. Alexa was a woman happy with her career, herself, her life. And Cam had no business thinking about her in any manner except as an aunt to his sons.

Besides, she might be here to spy on him for the Barrington grandparents who wanted to take his sons away from him. He had to remain on his guard. Now was not the time to let a sexy pair of legs distract him.

"Have you started your medical practice yet?" Alexa asked.

Was her question just friendly curiosity? Or was she gathering information to be used against him in court?

"I'm planning to start just as soon as the house is finished."

She frowned. "I thought Tyler told you it was ready to move into."

"My older brother's idea of a home is a roof to keep out the rain. He doesn't miss little conveniences like electricity and plumbing."

Cam swung onto Highview's main street, taking pleasure in the mountain range that had overlooked the whole of his childhood and youth, the great mountain chain spreading north and south of town for hundreds of miles. Highview nestled along the river in a quiet valley of lush grassland and rolling hills. The centerpiece of town was the Highview Hotel, built in the Victorian fashion and painted in soft gray and blue.

"I'll get you a room at the hotel."

"I really came to see the boys." Without creasing her designer suit, she turned to send the twins a fond glance, every hair on her head in place. "And I've camped out before."

"Where? In the lobby of the Waldorf-Astoria?" he teased.

"Try Nepal, Katmandu and Tanzania." She arched a perfectly plucked brow at him in challenge. "I'm tougher than I look."

He hadn't meant to offend her, could hear the hurt in her voice even as she dared him to send her to the hotel. "You look great."

She let out a delicate snort. "Why does that sound like an accusation, instead of a compliment?"

"Look, I'm sorry." He threaded his fingers through his hair with exasperation, knowing he should have been honest with her from the start. "My house isn't ready for visitors. I can't imagine you would be comfortable there."

"I've slept in *yurts* with the Mongols in Russia, in tents with nomads in the Sahara. They have the most fiery paintings of horses in Russia, and such delicate carvings in the desert." Her voice turned dreamy as she described the horsemanship captured in paintings so rich in detail that museums all over the world vied for them, and carvings of bones so ancient it was amazing they'd survived. Her passion for her finds and her work spoke to him on a level he understood. She felt about art the way he did about medicine. Ever since he'd been a kid, he'd wanted to be a doctor, couldn't imagine doing anything else.

As he swung into the fast-food restaurant's parking lot, he wondered what had brought her away from her work to Colorado. By the time the meal ended, she still hadn't answered his unspoken questions. They'd avoided grown-up talk, instead, both of them focusing on the boys. But sometime during the meal, they'd reached an unspoken truce, and he'd decided if she wanted to camp out at his house, she was more than welcome.

Alexa was good company, interesting, cheerful and easy on the eyes. He saw no reason not to enjoy the friendship or company she was offering.

The twins fell asleep during the ride back to the Sutton ranch. With the muddy driveway full of contractors' vehicles, Cam was forced to park near the barn. He turned to Alexa, who was looking around with lively curiosity. "If you'll stay with the boys, I'll see if the stone mason will move his truck out of the way."

"Sure." She glanced at the sleeping twins. "No problem."

THE MOMENT CAMERON disappeared behind the electric truck, Jason's eyes opened wide, the angelic look of sleep turning to mischievousness. Before Alexa could stop him, he tugged on Flynn's ear, waking his twin.

Jason kicked his feet. "Out."

"Out. Out. Out!" Flynn echoed.

They *had* been sitting a long time. She wouldn't mind stretching her legs and walking around, either.

Cam had told her to stay with the twins, but he hadn't said to stay in the vehicle. She'd noted and admired Cam's easy competence with his children, the love shining from his eyes whenever he glanced their way. He didn't seem the kind of father who'd mind a little change in plans. What could a short walk hurt?

"If you boys promise to hold my hand, I'll take you out."

Flynn pointed to the barn. "Can we ride our ponies?"

Alexa struggled with Jason's buckle. "We can go *look* at them." Flynn had his seat belt unfastened before she'd finished with his brother's, but she blocked him from exiting the vehicle with her body, determined not to lose him.

During the past year, she'd become comfortable with children, reading books on child care and offering to watch her friends' children. The effort had cost her, but she'd been determined to overcome her reluctance and fears. Eventually she'd put aside her unease and been paid back in happiness, which she'd only wished Sandra had lived long enough to see.

In a moment she had both boys by the hand. Their little legs pumped three times as fast as hers, eagerly pulling her toward the most magnificent barn she'd ever seen on any continent. From the outside, she could see the huge building was heated and air-conditioned, immaculately landscaped with an array of wildflowers amid the verdant grasses and freshly painted yellow with golden shutters.

Flynn suddenly pulled up short. "Uh-oh."

"Holy cow!" Jason pointed.

Their excited voices shot Alexa's pulse into high gear. A humongous bull charged around the barn's corner. For an instant, Alexa froze, staring into the animal's wild eyes.

At the sight of them, the bull pulled up short, shook his huge horns and pawed the ground. Charged.

Adrenaline rushed through her, burning her stomach with fear. With a strength Alexa didn't know she had, she scooped both boys into her arms, dashed back toward the vehicle, opened the door. She shoved both shouting children to safety on the floor and slammed the door. There was no time to climb in after them.

Horns aimed low, the bull head-butted the SUV, missing Alexa by inches, denting the passenger's front door, lifting the vehicle several inches off the ground. Then he turned toward her, about to charge again, possibly tip over the vehicle.

His head was down, his horns pointed her way. In horror, she visualized him crushing the kids, kicking in windows with those massive hind quarters and deadly hooves.

She had to protect the children. From her peripheral vision, she saw Cameron racing to the vehicle. He wouldn't arrive in time.

She had to do something now.

Something fast.

In Spain she'd been disgusted by matadors waving red capes at bulls to get them to charge. In a flash, Alexa realized her suit was cherry red. Tearing at her jacket buttons in renewed panic, Alexa whipped off the bright red garment and flung it aside—away from the vehicle. Just as she'd prayed, the bull changed direction, charging the flash of red, catching the material on its horns, then stomping it into the ground.

Slowly she moved toward the vehicle's door to check the twins. Her spiked heel snapped. Alexa tripped. At the cracking sound, the animal first raised his head, then lowered his thick neck, aiming the wicked horns at her. It was too late to remove her skirt. Too late to open the dented front door and climb inside. And if she stayed where she was, the babies would be at risk.

She had to move.

Shifting sideways, she raced away from the children, slipped in the mud, rolled. The animals' hooves pounded the ground. Alexa scrambled, crawling and kicking through the mud to her feet.

She turned, looked over her shoulder. The bull was close enough for her to see the whites of his eyes, feel his hot breath on her neck.

Chapter Two

"Fall and roll!"

At Cameron's shout, Alexa flung herself sideways, spinning through puddles and mud. Once she was out of his gun sight, Cameron fired the .410 shotgun pistol he'd just removed from his locked gloved compartment. As his gun discharged at the bull, Alexa kept rolling, a swirl of flashing red and mud.

At the pepper spray of pellets striking his hide, the angry bull bellowed in surprise and halted midstride. The wide-spread shot hadn't penetrated the bull's thick hide, and as several ranch hands herded him toward the paddock he'd escaped from, Cam turned to Alexa.

When he'd pulled the gun out of the SUV, he'd done a quick check of the twins, and they were fine. But Alexa was lying unnaturally still. He prayed the red he could see was material from her skirt and not blood.

"Dr. Cam, I'll take the boys up to the house," Cody Barnes offered with a shy look. The lanky young ranch hand was accustomed to watching his mother's brood, and often filled in for Cam if he got busy. Cam nodded, grateful. Cody would reassure the twins, tell them cowboy stories and make them forget their scare while Cam attended to Alexa.

"Thanks," Cam said, and ran toward Alexa, his heart pounding against his ribs with fear that she'd sustained a mortal injury. "Bodine, fetch my bag from the house."

Bodine Stone, the head foreman, was accustomed to taking orders from Rafe, but he didn't object to Cam's hurried plea. "Where in the house, Doc?"

"Under my desk."

Cam took one deep breath to steady himself. Although he was a trained physician, taking care of Alexa was very different from treating a stranger. Cam still felt guilty that he hadn't saved Sandra. If only he'd been with her on his day off—instead of at a seminar. If only he could have put all his medical skills to use on the person he loved more than anyone else. He still blamed himself that he hadn't even been at the hospital when she'd arrived in the ambulance. Maybe if he'd been there, he could have done... something. He hadn't even gotten the chance to hold her hand. Or kiss her goodbye. It took all his objectivity and medical training to put the past from his mind. Put the last horrific minutes from his mind.

A patient needed him, and he would remain detached to do his job. Kneeling beside Alexa, he smoothed aside silky black hair caked with mud and felt for the pulse at her neck. Relief flooded through him. Her pulse was good. Strong and steady.

Gently he turned her onto her back to check her breathing. She immediately started to cough up mud and spit out dirt. Finally he heard the sound he'd been waiting for—her gasp for air.

"Easy. The wind's been knocked out of you." He knelt at her side and ran his hands over her limbs but found no obvious broken bones. He searched the rest of her for signs of injury. "Don't move."

"The twins?" Her eyes brimmed with tears.

He found no sign the bull had gored her and realized with relief she would be fine. That her first thought was for his sons' well-being sent his objectivity flying and his admiration spiraling. Alexa wasn't just another pretty face. She had spunk and courage and as much moxie as any rodeo clown who risked his life to save endangered bull riders. And she smelled better. Much better. In spite of the mud, the expensive perfume she wore was doing strange things to his thoughts, making it difficult to concentrate.

"The boys are fine."

She coughed and turned her head to spit out a little more dirt. Her color beneath the mud was too pale, her chest heaved with spasms, her body convulsed for air. And still she asked about the boys. "You're sure?"

"Yes. Don't try to talk yet. Relax. Give your body a moment to recover."

Bodine shoved the physician's bag into his hands. "Here, Doc."

"Thanks." Cam extracted sterile water, wet some gauze and gently wiped Alexa's face free of mud. First he cleaned around eyes that were still wide and frightened, then her aristocratic nose, which flared at his touch, and finally her mouth, which trembled as she tried to contain the aftermath of her fear.

Her entire body shook. "I'm sorry I took the twins out of the—"

"Shh. Not another word. No way could you have expected a bull to charge you." He caressed her hair, using his most reassuring tone, his voice husky with the rash of emotions pouring through him at what could have happened. "You saved my boys' lives. If not for your quick thinking..." He swallowed the lump that had suddenly risen in his throat. Alexa had risked her life to draw the bull away from the twins, and he owed her a debt he could never repay. The boys were his living legacy from Sandra, their hope for the future. The idea of anything happening to them was unbearable.

He shut down the thought. He had no business worrying about his own problems when a patient needed him. "Do you hurt anywhere?"

"Everywhere." Alexa let out an unladylike groan. "I feel like a wrestler who just got body-slammed. But I don't think it's anything serious. Just bumps and bruises."

"Any sharp pains?"

"*Nada.*"

"How's your vision?"

"Now that the dirt's clearing from my eyeballs, you don't look so fuzzy."

"Did you bang your head? Any numbness in your hands or feet?"

Alexa pushed herself to a sitting position. "I'm fine." She looked down at her silk blouse, which had once been a pristine white, and grimaced with distaste. "Or I will be fine after I've had a hot soak and…"

She must have caught the look of "no can do" on Cameron's face. Just before the bull had interrupted his conversation, Cam had learned from the plumber that the water line wouldn't be hooked to the house today. The swimming pool would remain empty, and they'd continue to drink bottled water. One of the trucks had slid off the muddy driveway into the open ditch, crushing the PVC pipe. Another delay.

"I could take you up to the Senator's house."

"Not looking like a pig who wallowed in mud, you won't."

"The Senator won't care—especially after I tell him how you saved his grandsons."

"I care." She started to place a pleading hand on his arm, saw all the mud and pulled back. "Can you hook a hose up to the unbroken part of the water line?"

Cam couldn't believe his ears. The woman had faced down a bull with the courage of a matador, and she was worried about someone seeing her with a little mud on her face? To her credit, she hadn't complained, only offered suggestions.

Cam humored her, sure she would change her mind. "You want to wash with a hose?"

He took Alexa's hand, helping her to her feet. She squared her shoulders and tilted her chin to look up at him. "Is there another choice?"

"The Highview Hotel—"

"No."

"Well, we wash the twins in the horse trough. But I don't think you'll fit," he teased lightly.

Her eyes flared. At first he thought with anger. But when she ópened her fingers and flicked mud droplets at him, he realized she was amused, laughing at her ruined designer suit, laughing at the mud, laughing with relief that the twins were okay. That she was okay.

Several ranch hands hovered around. Bodine stepped forward. ''You need any help with the hose, Doc?''

''See if you can rig up a makeshift shower out by the barn and bring towels and soap,'' he said, keeping hold of Alexa's hand just in case she slipped or was more injured than he thought. Her hand with those perfectly manicured nails encrusted with mud felt so small in his, yet there was strength in those fingers. He recalled her ripping off her jacket, flinging it aside. His breathing had almost stopped as he'd prayed her ruse would work and give him time to retrieve his gun.

She'd survived and now he hoped shock hadn't hidden any internal injuries. ''How do you feel?''

''Muddy.'' She kept hold of his hand and surveyed the driveway. ''What was that bull doing in your front yard?''

Good point. ''Either he broke out of the paddock…''

''Or?''

''Someone didn't bar the gate properly.''

She looked around warily as if expecting the bull to charge again. ''Do animals get loose often?''

He squeezed her hand gently but couldn't control the hardness in his tone. ''It's never happened before, and if I find out who the careless S.O.B. was, I'll knock his ears down so fast they'll do for wings."

She shot him an odd look. "Excuse me?"

"I'd hit him so hard he couldn't answer St. Peter's questions."

"You talk funny when you're riled."

"You could have been killed." With one finger, he tipped up her chin, looked directly into eyes as green as the San Juan Mountains. "I'll never forget what you did. I don't know how to thank you."

She cocked her head to the side. "I can think of a way."

Once again, she made him very aware she was a woman. It wasn't just her muddy white blouse molding her body like plastic wrap that had him noticing she had curves in all the right places, but her attitude. Her sassy reply and the glint of devilry in her eyes rocked him back onto his heels.

He didn't like the way she made him notice her. Not one damn bit. Not that he could blame Alexa for looking good. Healthy. Alive. But Sandra was still in his thoughts.

Rarely a day passed by where he still didn't reach for the phone to tell her an amusing annecdote or to remind her to pick something up for the twins. In his thoughts, in his dreams at night, Sandra was part of his life. And although logic told him she was dead, in his heart, he felt looking at another woman was a betrayal.

Crossing his arms over his chest, he eyed her warily. "What?"

Her eyes misted, surprising him as they turned a

soft, hazy sea-green. "You can help me keep a promise."

She started into the barn and he followed. So she was finally going to admit the reason she'd come. Had she promised her grandparents she'd try to convince him to give up the twins? If she thought he would capitulate to the Barringtons' demands to surrender custody of the boys, she'd miscalculated badly. Giving up his sons wasn't an option he would consider. Ever.

Perhaps he was misreading her intentions. Cam waited patiently, without jumping to further conclusions, leading her past the barn toward the exterior horse stalls. The woman had almost died saving his sons. He wasn't about to accuse her without hard information. Keeping his patience wasn't even a stretch, not when he really wanted to check her more carefully to reassure himself she was all right.

"Who did you promise?" he asked, stopping just outside the stall.

"Sandra." Alexa held eye contact with him as if by holding his stare, she could will him to believe her. "Before she died, Sandra made me promise her that the boys would never be raised by nannies or sent off to a boarding school."

Surprise and doubt must have flickered in his expression. "I have no intention of—"

"But my grandparents do."

Suddenly the reason for Alexa's unexpected visit focused like a microscope's lens. The woman was just full of surprises, and he felt shamed by his earlier suspicions. "You came here to help me?"

Alexa left him behind, entering the stall and talking while she stripped and threw her muddy clothing over the top of the door. Cameron had inherited the barn along with acre upon acre of rich pasture land after his father had divided up the ranch among his sons. None of the brothers had yet built their own barns, so all of them kept their horses here.

It might be the ultimate in barns, but Cam couldn't believe Alexa could so contentedly shower here. This was where the grooms washed down the animals before leading them into their stalls. Thick wooden slats lent Alexa some privacy, but the cracks were wide enough to get an eyeful if a man stood close enough.

Cameron turned his back—although Alexa didn't seem overly concerned by his presence. She must figure he was immune to nudity because he was a doctor.

But he was also a man. A man with burgeoning needs and whetted desires. Was it just his time to awaken from more than a year of mourning? Or was something inside him responding to Alexa Whitfield on a level he couldn't assess? As a man of science, Cameron Sutton no more believed in instantaneous love than he believed in little green men. Yet he couldn't deny the heat in his loins as he listened to her speak over the shower, imagined the cool droplets sluicing away the mud to reveal pink skin, slender curves and those long, long legs. And he fought hard to suppress the image, an image that didn't belong there.

"Sandra's last words should pull weight with a judge." Alexa spoke as if oblivious to the fact that only a few rails of wood and his honor were all that protected her from his eager gaze.

But his imagination left him no peace as he envisioned Alexa raising her hands to shampoo her hair, back arching delicately, face spattered with water droplets. Forcing himself to concentrate on her words, instead of the erotic images in his mind, he broke into a light sweat.

The hearing wasn't for another week. "The judge may not let you speak. I'm sure any good attorney will claim your testimony is hearsay."

"Exceptions are made when the children's mother is deceased."

"You've consulted a lawyer?"

She must have heard his incredulous tone, for she responded with a self-assurance that surprised him. "Don't you understand the enormity of what's at stake? I assure you my grandparents will spare no expense to win custody. They'll arrive with a barrage of attorneys to fight you."

"I've never understood why they would contest a father's custody. They're your grandparents. Aren't they too old to raise children?"

Cameron really wasn't too concerned. His very competent attorney had assured him that a judge wouldn't favor the great-grandparents over the father unless some very unusual circumstances prevailed— like the father being committed to a mental institution or convicted of a crime.

The hose finally stopped running, and he heard her drag a towel off the rails and the swish as material wrapped around her body. He pictured the towel's corner tucked between her breasts, above several inches of bare thighs and shapely calves, and decided not to turn around.

"The issue isn't age. It's money."

"I don't understand."

"You mean you don't know?"

At the sharp edge in her voice, Cameron turned, despite his intention not to. "Don't know what?"

With her hair slicked back off her face, water droplets spiking her eyelashes and the soft pink towel clinging to more curves than he'd remembered, his mouth went dry.

"Our great-grandfather was Arthur Levenger. Ever hear of him?"

"Of course." He strove to keep his voice at a conversational level. The woman had no idea how she was affecting his pulse rate. "Wasn't he one of America's last great robber barons, the industrialist who made a fortune in the shipping and oil industries during the last part of the nineteenth-century?"

She raised her arms and twisted excess water out of her hair. He swallowed hard, waiting for the towel to fall, but she'd secured it well, and he didn't know whether to be relieved or disappointed.

She reached into the bag a ranch hand had carried for her from the SUV and opened a jar of cream. Slowly she dabbed it on her arms, her elbows, her wrists, working it into her skin as she spoke. "Old Arthur set aside an enormous trust fund. While he ensured an ample legacy for his heirs, Levenger's will stated that the first *male* heirs would inherit the majority of his vast wealth."

He watched her sit sideways on a bench and

smooth the cream over her toes, calves and ankles as if she was in a boudoir, not a horse stall. "So?"

"The interest has been compounding for over a century and the estate has been overseen by the shrewdest Wall Street investors."

"And?" How could he concentrate when he found her every movement provocative?

"Your sons are the first male heirs since the old codger died. Do you understand what I'm saying?"

"I'm not that interested in financial matters." He much preferred flesh and bones, genteel bones with creamy skin, although he didn't dare say so. Not when the flesh was so temptingly damp, pink and glowing. Not when the bones were aristocratic and reminded him of delicate sculptures. Not when he had no business looking at her.

"Your sons are two of the richest little boys in the United States."

Her words shocked him from his lustful thinking. Cam wasn't sure how he felt about her revelation, but he knew it would change his sons' lives in significant ways. While the Sutton family was wealthy in its own right and as a medical doctor he earned a good living, different kinds of wealth, spectacular wealth, came with a new set of problems. That kind of money made his sons a target for con men, kidnappers and terrorists, and debutantes.

Some day it would give the twins choices he wasn't sure he wanted them to have. But he still didn't understand the whole picture. "Your grandparents are already rich. What does the inheritance have to do with my boys?"

"Until the boys reach the age of twenty-one, whoever has custody of the Levenger heirs administers the trust fund.''

Cam knew that vast wealth equated to power, but he still didn't understand the full implications—not until Alexa laid it out for him as she towel-dried her hair.

''The trust endows the arts, charities, medical research and makes political contributions. Whoever controls the trust has enormous power.''

''Why didn't Sandra tell me?''

She didn't know. ''Until recently, I didn't know, either.''

''Power is what your grandparents want?''

''Power is what they don't want to relinquish.'' At his frown, Alexa paused in the braid she was twisting her hair into. ''Apparently our grandparents administered the funds and never told Sandra about it. But that duty now belongs to you. Or it will, once the custody is finalized.''

''My attorney doesn't think I can lose the boys.''

''Don't be so sure.''

His gut churned, but he didn't let his anger or suddenly rising fear show. Instead, he forced patience into his tone. ''What do you mean?''

''Suppose the Barringtons' lawyer proves you're unfit?''

Despite his determination to remain patient, he couldn't keep the growl out of his tone. ''And just how would they do that?''

Alexa faced him, her eyes sympathetic, her words hard. ''You're raising your children in the wilds of Colorado, on a ranch.''

"They can't take my kids from me because we live in Colorado."

"You're a busy medical doctor who almost lost his children to a loose bull..."

Was Alexa threatening him? Warning him? Or just showing him how a smart lawyer could twist things in court? Before Alexa's arrival, Cam hadn't realized the stakes. He'd thought the battle was over his sons, not his sons and their trust fund.

Should he bargain with the Barringtons? Give them control of the fund if they'd agree to drop the custody battle? Cam didn't care a flying fig about administering the trust, but was it fair to his boys to give away control of their inheritance?

"Cam?"

"Yeah?"

"You're awfully quiet."

"You've given me a lot to think about."

"Well, think about this." At the sharp edge in her tone, he paid close attention. "Could someone have set that bull loose to discredit your parenting ability?"

For a moment he wondered if the scare had addled her thinking, seeing conspiracies where none existed. But she'd been too logical, too methodical in leading this conversation where she wanted him to go for him to believe she was overreacting out of fear. He sought to reassure her.

"Most likely a hand forgot to bar the gate."

"But it could have been left open deliberately, couldn't it?" The way she kept insisting the accident had been intentional sent a chill down his spine. That little stunt could have cost her and his boys their lives.

Still, he couldn't buy her line of reasoning. Setting the bull loose was like firing a gun without aiming. No one could have predicted where a loose bull would go or whom it would attack. True, Alexa had been wearing a flapping red skirt, but how could anyone have known that before she'd arrived?

Unless someone had seen her at the airport and driven to the ranch while they'd eaten burgers in town.

Cameron looked around uneasily, wondering if someone was spying on him this minute, taking pictures with a telephoto lens.

"If my sons don't survive—" he could barely speak the words "—who controls the trust?"

Alexa's face paled. "My grandparents. But I don't think they would resort to…"

"Murder?"

Chapter Three

Cameron couldn't believe how long it took Alexa to dry herself, dress and accompany him to the house, although he had to admit she was worth waiting for. He didn't expect a woman who seemed comfortable showering in a horse stall to be such a perfectionist about her appearance. He couldn't decide whether to be annoyed or fascinated, especially when he was anxious to check in on the twins. Soothing his impatience by telling himself the hands would shout from the house at any sign of trouble, he paced, waiting for Alexa.

Finally she joined him and he took her suitcase. She had twisted her hair into some kind of fancy braid that showed off the delicate diamonds in her ears and the lovely arch of her neck. She'd reapplied makeup, and her glossy pink lips now matched a pastel shirt, form-fitting cream slacks and sandals. She'd even switched purses to match her shoes. He supposed he should be grateful she hadn't made him wait so she could reapply matching nail polish, too.

As he walked alongside her, however, he couldn't

help appreciating the reapplication of her exotic perfume. And his mouth watered.

Uncomfortable with his thoughts about Alexa, uncomfortable with the suspicions she'd planted in his head, he broke the silence, striving for normalcy. "You've become comfortable with children."

Her lips turned up with pleasure. "I've been practicing."

For children of her own? So there *was* someone special in her life. Although he couldn't imagine Alexa giving up her life of constant traveling, perhaps she'd found a househusband amenable to staying home with children while she was away. He didn't know why the thought of her finding someone bothered him, but it did.

Seemingly unaware of his disapproval, she strode by his side, her long legs having no trouble keeping up. "Sandra once told me if I didn't try with children, I'd never learn. So this past year, I've been reading every book I could get my hands on, practicing on my friends' kids. I was surprised to have so much fun."

"They can be a hell of a lot of work, too. The way you handled Flynn and Jason, I'd say you're now a pro."

"I started learning because Sandra dared me." Alexa stopped walking and looked at him. "Does it bother you when I talk about her?"

The direct question took him aback. Alexa's forthrightness kept catching him by surprise, and he found his respect for her upping another notch. He kept forgetting that behind the delicious-looking package was a woman with keen intelligence.

"Actually I find the memories comforting." Still, Cameron made an effort to turn the conversation back to Alexa. "So are you taking Sandra's advice and getting married? Raising a few kids of your own?"

Alexa frowned at him with as much confusion as if he were a three-headed calf. "Where'd you get that idea?"

He thought he heard a flicker of pain in the sharpness of her tone and didn't understand what caused it. "I'm sorry. I just assumed you were preparing..."

"I was preparing for my next visit with the twins."

From the closed look on her face, Cam knew he'd touched a nerve. He didn't pry. They started walking again in silence, but he refused to let it go on too long.

"Sandra hated this ranch. She always called it primitive, but I thought the boys would grow strong out here. I want them to come to love this place as much as I do."

Alexa surveyed the muddy driveway, the puddles, and then raised her eyes past the house to the verdant sun-drenched valley, the towering mountains, and breathed deeply. "There's a peacefulness here you can't find in the city." She turned to him, her mood changing with lightning swiftness. "But if you think for one moment I'm walking through that mud..."

He restrained a chuckle. "It's the only way to get to the house."

"One mud bath a day is enough for any woman." She stepped closer and placed her hands on his shoulders. "So carry me?"

There was no sexual innuendo in her tone, her demeanor or her actions. And yet every nerve in Cam's body went on full alert. He didn't want to touch that skin, flushed, creamed and perfumed after her shower. He didn't want to hold her close enough for her to feel his heart racing. He didn't want to think of her as a woman. He didn't want to want her.

But he'd be a cad to refuse her simple request. She was a tiny woman with a delicate frame. But lifting her into his arms wasn't effortless. How could it be when it took all his effort to steady his breathing, to act as if he couldn't feel the soft curve of her breast against his chest and the wisps of silky hair that had escaped her braid teasing his neck?

She placed her arms around his neck, and he started along the driveway knowing that after holding her in his arms, he'd go to bed tonight wondering what would have happened if he'd lowered his mouth to hers. And damning himself for his urges. Although Cam wasn't pleased by his newly awakened interest in the opposite sex, the timing could have been better; the woman could have been someone more appropriate.

Alexa was not for him. She was Sandra's cousin. A woman who traveled the world for her career. She was direct and sassy and trouble. He told himself not to look at her, not to breathe in her scent, not to think how good she felt in his arms.

He would react this way to any woman. He'd simply neglected certain needs too long.

He was lying to himself. He didn't know how, but she'd kindled an ember from the ashes of his heart.

Those glossy pink lips were irresistible. Impulsively he lowered his head until their mouths were inches apart. He felt her quick shiver in his arms, saw a flicker of surprise and need in her eyes, knew she could avoid his mouth if she wished. Instead, he saw interest blaze, a spark flare, which fueled him on.

He nibbled softly at her upper lip. Once. Twice. When that teasing taste warmed his blood, he crushed his hungry mouth to hers.

He'd been prepared for her to turn her head away, mutter a protest, or scream, or scratch, or slap. And he would have stopped, forced himself to be satisfied with just a quick sample. Although he'd once been a man of large appetites, he took no pleasure in forcing himself on an unwilling woman.

He'd been quite unprepared for Alexa to willingly kiss him back, creating an explosion of impressions. Searing. Sunny. Sensational. She was kissing him with a hunger that matched his own. Her arms wound around his neck and into his hair, drawing his head closer.

And their mouths fit perfectly, her lips giving and giving and giving. She radiated passion, warmth, desire, inflaming him and drawing him deeper.

A hot kittenish moan at the back of her throat demanded and surrendered. She wrapped herself tighter to him, her soft curves pressing against him, shooting waves of fire to his core.

"Ahem." The interruption came from outside the web of passion she'd woven around them.

"Go away," Cam muttered.

Alexa's hands suddenly slammed into his chest, and Cam looked up to see his brother Chase sitting on a horse and looking down at them with sheer mischief in his eyes. "I hate to interrupt."

"Then don't," Cameron growled, his thoughts hazy, dipping his head to reclaim those soft voluptuous lips.

"Stop." Alexa's hand pressed him back. "I said no."

Chase chuckled. "You'll have to forgive him—he's out of practice."

Hot blood pulsing through his veins made patience impossible. Cameron could have strangled his brother, would get rid of him as soon as he got his breath back, as soon as his hands were free.

In truth, he was angrier with himself than his brother. As the sensual haze cleared and he realized what he'd just done, Cam knew he'd mostly himself to blame for his actions. He'd been the one unable to halt his impulse to kiss her. He'd been the one who'd forgotten that Alexa had just gotten off the plane this morning and almost been killed. He'd taken advantage of her vulnerability.

Cam took most of the blame on his shoulders but the woman in his arms had to share some of it too. She could have turned her head away from his kiss. But she hadn't.

Even now heat rose to Alexa's cheeks as she peered at Chase, who tipped his hat. "Chase Sutton."

"Alexa Whitfield." Although Cam still held her tightly against his chest, she held out her hand to his brother. "This is crazy. I wasn't kissing him."

Chase raised her hand to his lips and kissed her

wrist—no doubt to annoy Cam. "I wish I wasn't getting kissed like that."

"I'll tell Laura you said so," Cam warned.

Chase's eyebrows rose, and he immediately dropped Alexa's hand. Cam's brother genuinely adored his wife and sons, and Cam would never follow through on his threat. But keeping Chase on his toes came as naturally as breathing.

Alexa refused to meet Cam's gaze. "Cameron took me by surprise. I had no idea, he would… I'm not interested," she explained weakly.

Cam eyed her skeptically. "Then why were you kissing me back?"

Alexa sputtered, radiating indignance. "You… you—"

"—Look, I hate to interrupt such an interesting discussion," Chase said, "and you can be sure Laura will want details when I get back, but I didn't ride over here for the air—however hot it may be," he teased, then turned serious gray eyes on Cam. "Keith's running a fever and Laura wants you to take a look at him."

Cam shook his head to clear it, trying hard to think. "We've had a little trouble around here. I hate to leave the twins."

"I'll watch them," Alexa volunteered.

Still carrying Alexa, Cam started walking toward the house, and his brother stayed mounted as he walked his horse beside them. "I don't know if that's a good idea."

Alexa huffed. "You don't trust me?"

Cam explained to Chase about the loose bull and finished summing up by the time they arrived at the front porch. Cam eagerly set Alexa back on her feet, anxious to break the connection between them but missing the feel of her in his arms.

Chase rubbed his chin. ''I'd bring Keith to you, but I don't want the twins to catch anything. Why don't I have some of the hands come in from the pasture and work close by? Alexa can phone if there's a problem.''

Nodding in agreement as they walked inside, Cam grabbed his bag. ''How high is Keith's temperature?''

''A hundred and three.''

Alexa looked around the unfinished house, her eyes curious. ''You *live* here?''

His thoughts already on his nephew, Cameron ignored the lack of furniture, drywall, plumbing and electricity. ''I told you it wasn't done. I'll take you to the hotel after I get back.''

Alexa didn't seem to hear him. She peeked into the kitchen—or what would be the kitchen, once appliances and cabinets arrived. ''I love the beautiful tongue-and-groove oak ceiling. Mind if I rearrange a few things? Oversee your workers?''

What could it hurt? Cam didn't have a knack for overseeing construction, and he knew it. And he hated dealing with hired help. However, the house was much closer to completion than it looked. One pipe connection would hook up water to the finished sinks, showers and hot water heater. All the electric wires had been run and just required attachment to the circuit box. The house lacked one window pane and the downstairs drywall could go up in a day. But the contractor gave him excuse after excuse. The plumber couldn't find the right parts, and the electrician never bothered to finish the job. A few ranch hands and the baby-sitter, Julie, were his only reliable help.

Before Cam could agree to letting Alexa baby-sit, his cook, Ray Potter, barreled into the room, mopping his sweating face with a red bandanna. His face flushed with anger, his bushy eyebrows twitching, the cook exuded rage that blasted everyone in the room.

Beads of sweat dribbled from Ray's forehead to his jowled cheek. "The contractor promised I'd have a kitchen by now." The cook pointed at Cam. "You promised I wouldn't be working under these primitive conditions for more than a week. Well, it's been a month, and I don't have a refrigerator or a stove or a sink. You have me outside in this heat, cooking over a camp stove. It's bad for my blood pressure. Bad for my heart. I quit."

Amusement twinkled in Alexa's eyes as the cook turned on his heel and huffed out of the house. To give her credit, she didn't crack a smile.

Cameron supposed Alexa couldn't make a mess of setting up a household any worse than he had. "Feel free to take over. Make yourself at home."

Alexa nodded. "I'll just check in on Cody and the twins, and then talk to your contractor."

"Uh-huh." Glad to leave the entire situation in her hands, glad to put some physical distance between them, Cam checked his medical bag, making sure he had several antibiotic samples. Keith was prone to ear infections, but his temperature didn't usually run so high.

Alexa's soft voice interrupted his thoughts. "I might buy a few things. Groceries. A shower curtain, drapes."

"Fine. Use the phone to order, and ask Cody to pick up your purchases in town." Cam snapped his bag shut and grabbed a hat off the door. "My cell phone number's nailed on the kitchen wall. Call if you need me."

Alexa snapped her fingers. "Not so fast, Doctor."

Her words stopped him and he turned to see a mischievous glint in her eye as she held out her hand to him, palm up. "You're forgetting that I need something."

Beside him, Chase restrained a smile as if he could read Alexa's mind. Cam didn't have a clue.

Slightly annoyed Chase knew something he didn't and irritated she was delaying him with talk about the sad state of construction when he needed to examine Keith and return quickly, he restrained an impulse to snap at her.

"What do you need?"

"Your credit card."

"You don't have one?" he couldn't resist asking, knowing full well how wealthy Alexa was.

"It's your house."

Cam opened his wallet and tossed it to her, anxious to be on his way. He'd avoided buying stuff. He hated making the decisions about the house when he was itching to open his medical practice. Besides, how much damage could one woman do with a credit card in just a few hours?

FOUR HOURS LATER, Alexa felt satisfied with the work she'd accomplished. Cameron's house had a masculine architecture that simply needed a woman's touch to make it home—that is, if the contractor ever finished the construction. Soaring ceilings and floor-to-ceiling windows invited the magnificent view inside.

Now all the house needed was drywall, flooring, interior carpentry, electrical hookups and plumbing. Then the real work of interior decorating could begin. Alexa couldn't help imagining how she would emphasize the massive stone fireplace with a Moulie, the only living artist to hang in the Louvre. But art should have been the last thing on her mind.

Cody had been wonderfully helpful, the lanky ranch hand bringing the groceries, furniture and supplies she'd ordered from town into the kitchen where she stacked the smaller items in the doorless pantry. She'd put Cameron's credit card to good use, and all afternoon, every time she thought of that kiss he'd stolen, she'd taken pleasure in running up his bill.

Damn him! Whatever had possessed the man to kiss her? She hadn't flirted. She hadn't been interested. For years, Cameron Sutton had belonged to Sandra and only Sandra. He'd loved her cousin, been good to her, fathered her children. And not once had Alexa ever thought of Cameron as anything but a good man, a fine catch for Sandra. But one kiss had changed everything. One kiss had knocked her socks off and she still hadn't recovered. Every time she thought about that kiss, her pulse raced. Every time she thought about that kiss, her blood heated. Every time she thought about that kiss, she got angry, confused and embarrassed all over again. Talk about dy-

namite. His kiss had been pure Fourth of July
fireworks—the red-hot kind, with sparks that rocked
almost every belief she'd ever had about men and
women.

Alexa didn't believe in chemical attraction that ig-
nited with a simple kiss. She didn't believe in falling
for a tall, dark and handsome man who so obviously
needed a wife and would undoubtedly want more
children. And she certainly hadn't come out West for
an affair with her nephews' daddy. Sandra's husband.

Yet, kisses that marvelous didn't happen to Alexa.
She didn't even dream about kisses that marvelous.
She couldn't figure out exactly what had happened
to make her forget everything except Cameron Sutton.

As much as she'd denied her actions, she *had*
kissed him back. She hadn't wanted to admit it to
him, and even now she didn't want to admit it to
herself. Alexa kept telling herself she wouldn't think
about that kiss, wouldn't think about Cameron—not
as a man with eyes of pure sterling and gilded with
silver light. Or with lips that had made her so aware
she was a woman.

But as the afternoon wore on and she called the
general contractor, electrician and plumber while
keeping an eye on the twins, she discovered that her
resolution to forget that kiss was impossible.

If she hadn't promised Sandra to look after the
twins, she'd have been tempted to leave the moment
Cameron returned. But one kiss, no matter how devastating, wouldn't make her go back on her promise
to her cousin.

Cody Barnes brought in the last sack of groceries and set them by her feet. "What should I do with the rest, ma'am?"

When she looked at Cody, he blushed. She ignored his high color, suspecting the young man would have been more comfortable outside with the other ranch hands. He might have even taken some teasing about helping with the twins, yet he hadn't complained. Alexa couldn't help noticing that Cody kept looking out the front window, seemingly anxious for Julie to return from class.

Alexa left the groceries and spied through the window the pickup truck piled high with her credit-card purchases. While she instructed the lanky hand, she caught him watching a car pull in down the road. As the blond-haired, brown-eyed Julie exited her car, Cody followed the coed's every move. Obviously he had a crush on the children's baby-sitter.

Alexa kept the knowledge to herself, knowing a comment would just embarrass the young man. "Please place the grill on the patio and find someone to hook up the propane tank. For now, we can use the pool furniture inside."

Two hours later, Alexa looked around with weary satisfaction, grateful that Julie had returned to occupy and feed the twins so she could keep working on the house. The cheerful college student had the twins on her lap and had just finished reading them a story.

Flynn tugged Julie's hair. "Pretty."

Julie laughed and kissed the top of the little boy's head. "All right, buster. Why are you trying to butter me up?" When she spied Alexa watching her, she gestured for her to join them on the floor. "You have to watch out with these fellas. If they give you a compliment, that means they are about to ask for something they aren't supposed to have.''

Jason grinned and played with Julie's hair, too. "*Is* pretty.''

Alexa settled cross-legged on the rug that Cody had spread before the uncompleted fireplace. Julie, with a loving smile, gently tugged her hair out of reach. "Can you imagine these two heartbreakers at eighteen or twenty?''

"I'm sure every Harvard coed will be after them.''

Julie raised a blond eyebrow. "Harvard?''

"Sandra took out one of those prepaid tuition plans when they were born.''

"Wow! That's really awesome.'' The phone rang, and Julie turned to her charges, who were both fighting sleep and actually sitting still for a change. "Well, you guys had better be smart enough to attend an Ivy League school. And smart boys need their sleep.''

She gathered them up amid drowsy protests while Alexa answered the phone. "Hello.''

"I'll be back within half an hour,'' Cam's soft drawl purred through the phone lines.

"How's Keith?''

"Fever's down. I needed to watch him for a while before deciding whether to give him an antibiotic. But he's fighting off the infection on his own and the little tyke's going to be just fine.'' Just then, one of the twins let out a piercing whoop. "You managing okay?''

"We're fine.''

"Julie usually leaves for her dorm around eight.

Ask her to stay with you until I get home. I don't like the idea of you and the boys being alone.''

While she appreciated his concern, she hardly thought Julie could protect her. Besides, Alexa had traveled the world, and while she didn't carry a six-shooter in her purse or a knife in her garter, she'd managed alone for more years than she cared to admit.

Changing the subject, Alexa twisted the phone cord around her finger. Despite her work this afternoon, she'd taken the time to change her nail polish to a soft pink. Looking good gave her courage, and she might need all the courage she could muster after Cameron realized how much of his money she'd spent.

Suddenly a little nervous and a lot guilty, she blurted, ''I may have gone a little overboard with your credit card today.''

''It's all right. I may not be as wealthy as your grandparents, but I'm not exactly poor. I'm a doctor, remember?''

His voice had a caressing quality that made her distinctly uneasy, since it brought back another vivid reminder of their kiss. Electricity had sparked through her. Perhaps she should take him up on his offer to stay at the hotel in town. She wasn't sure she trusted herself alone with him in this house.

By the time Cam returned thirty minutes later, she'd almost made up her mind to leave, but one look at his exhausted face, his dark eyes crinkling at the corners from weariness, and she knew she'd be selfish to make him drive her into Highview at this late hour. He really looked beat.

"Was treating Keith that difficult?"

He shot her a wry grin. "The vet's on vacation and one of Rafe's mares went into labor. I kept telling him I'm an MD, not a veterinarian, but he wouldn't take no for an answer. I don't know which was worse, calming the mare who kept trying to kick me or calming my brother who kept threatening to punch me."

"He *didn't!*"

"He would have if I'd tried to leave. He considers the horses his children."

Cam spied the contemporary rugs, a mixture of jute and wool, scattered across the bare plywood subflooring. They lent a rich texture to the foyer, and he carefully wiped the mud off his shoes on the new mat she'd purchased. He visibly perked up as he entered the kitchen and surveyed the wrought-iron breakfast bar and wine rack in the corner with two comfortable leather-seat stools that slipped out of the way when not in use. Wrought-iron pot racks hung from the ceiling by double hooks holding a shiny collection of hammered copper pots with riveted brass handles.

"I left all our old stuff in Boston. Haven't gotten around to buying new furnishings."

"Julie told me."

"You've done wonders."

Alexa walked with him into the kitchen, not quite daring to tell him what she'd ordered from the store's catalogues to be delivered tomorrow. She took encouragement from the fact that at least he seemed to like the changes she'd made so far. "Have you eaten? Would you like something to—?"

A loud scream from outside chilled Alexa to the bone. "Julie!"

Cam's gaze turned in the direction of the stairs. He was clearly torn between running upstairs to see to the safety of the boys and sprinting outside.

"Go!" Alexa pushed him toward the door. "I'll check the boys."

She grabbed a flashlight and hurried upstairs, staying close to the wall to avoid falling on the banisterless staircase that a carpenter had promised to finish tomorrow. At least the second story had drywall and was mostly finished. She hurried into the boys' bedroom and aimed the flashlight at their beds. With relief, she saw they were still sound asleep, their chubby faces clean and cherubic-looking.

Quickly, Alexa checked the entire upstairs for intruders. Cam's room had only a rolled-up sleeping bag in one corner and open suitcase in the other. The other rooms were empty. She found nothing unusual except a kitten she suspected the boys had sneaked into the house. Picking up the lost animal in one hand, keeping the flashlight in the other, she returned downstairs to find Cam carrying Julie into the house.

Julie clutched Cam with fingers tight with tension. Her wide brown eyes brimmed with tears that she tried to blink away. Cam gently set her on the rug.

Alexa set down the kitten and hurried over, her mind teaming with questions. "What happened?"

Julie sniffed and stared at Cameron. "I was using the Porta Potti. When I came out, someone grabbed me from behind. I jabbed my elbow into him, and he threw me down."

"Did you see him?" Alexa asked as Cameron checked Julie's pupils with a penlight.

"I was so scared I just panicked. I think I screamed and fell, then everything went black. I opened my eyes...to find Cameron carrying me in here."

Alexa's neck prickled. "Did your attacker say anything?"

Julie shook her head and winced. "No."

"There isn't any blood." Cameron ran his fingers over Julie's head. "Does this hurt?"

"A little. I must have banged it when he threw me down."

Two near disasters in one day was just too much of a coincidence for Alexa. One look at the worry in Cam's eyes told her he was thinking the same thing. If someone had deliberately let the bull loose and that same someone had then attacked Julie, what could be his motive?

Robbery, rape, murder? Nothing made sense. And what could be the reason for attacking two different women? At a new thought, the hair on Alexa's neck prickled.

In the darkness, could the attacker have mistaken Julie for Alexa?

Chapter Four

Cameron called Noel Demory, Highview's sheriff, that night, and together they decided that his visit and investigation could wait until morning. Julie's friend, Leo Harley, had driven out to the ranch and taken her back to her dorm. Alexa had settled onto an air mattress in the guest room, and the rest of the night had passed peacefully.

The morning started at seven with a tempest of activity. Plumbers busily replaced the crushed water pipe. A loader filled in the dangerous ditch. The electrician actually thought he could hook up the wires to the circuit box and they might have electricity before dark. And despite the drywall shortage, a forklift unloaded pallets in the driveway, and carpenters busily tacked more drywall to the walls, covering the framing. Assistants followed behind with spackling tape and compound.

Alexa talked quietly to the workers, and the general contractor assured her the final window would be installed that afternoon. Cameron could have kissed her for putting his life back in order. But he wouldn't. Their one kiss had been too explosive.

Playing with dynamite wasn't his style. Right now, he and the twins needed stability, and Alexa would no doubt leave in the same manner she'd arrived, with little forethought and no warning.

Sheriff Noel Demory arrived at eight sharp. At five-foot-eight and 130 pounds, he made up in common sense what he lacked in bulk and stature. He'd helped Chase and Laura with a problem a while back and Cam thought he could help here too. Although the sheriff wasn't too ambitious and kept a low profile around town, he had a knack for preventing trouble before it started.

Despite her scare the night before, Julie, reliable as ever, had shown up on schedule, taking over her chores with the twins, insisting she'd rather work than have too much time on her hands to think. Alexa remained quiet, sipping the coffee Cody had brought over from the Senator's kitchen where his mother worked. The twins, incorrigible as ever, raced trucks through the living area.

As Cameron ushered the sheriff inside, Alexa and Julie each grabbed a twin and handed them over to Cody, who took them onto the back deck by the pool that was filling with water and out of hearing range. Cameron noted how the boy blushed whenever he neared either woman and wondered if the poor kid would ever overcome his painful shyness.

Not that he blamed the kid for feeling flustered. Julie oozed cowgirl sexuality in a stretchy T-shirt that bared her midriff and navel over low riding jeans. And Alexa's classy emerald blouse and cream slacks, belted at the waist, showed off her flawless figure. He restrained a smile when he noticed once again that she'd painted her nails a soft pearl color that matched a choker at her graceful neck.

The adults settled onto the pool furniture Alexa had purchased yesterday. First, Cameron recounted Alexa's encounter with the bull. Then the sheriff listened to Julie's story, taking notes and asking many of the same questions Alexa had last night.

Julie's answers remained consistent. Alexa looked thoughtful. The sheriff frowned at both women. "Have either of you dumped any boyfriends recently?"

Alexa and Julie both shook their heads.

"Maybe Cameron has an old girlfriend, someone jealous?" the sheriff asked.

Cameron set the record straight. "There was no one special before Sandra."

Julie sighed. "It was a man who attacked me."

"What makes you think so?" Alexa asked.

"The arm that grabbed me seemed…hard. Muscular. It was just an impression, nothing I can put my finger on."

The sheriff took notes. "Do you remember his scent?"

"Like aftershave?" Julie shook her head. "I'm sorry, I was just scared. It was so dark."

"Don't be silly." Alexa squeezed Julie's hand.

The sheriff turned to Cameron. "You fired anyone lately?"

"My cook, Ray Potter, quit yesterday."

Julie snapped her fingers. "In all the excitement, I forgot to tell you that my friend Leo would be happy to have the job. I told him to stop by this afternoon. Hope that's okay."

"I'll be happy to talk to him," Cameron said. He'd have the Senator look into Leo's background. With what had gone on around here, he wouldn't take any unnecessary chances. In fact, he might have his father run checks on all the new people.

"Let's look at the spot where Julie was attacked," the sheriff suggested.

Cameron had had another portable-toilet unit installed off the pool deck. "I did as you asked and roped off the area. No one's been there since last night."

"Good."

From her expression, Julie didn't relish the idea of returning to the crime scene. She walked outside, staying close to the sheriff. "What do you hope to find?"

"I'll dust the Porta Potti for fingerprints."

"Every construction worker on this site has likely been in there," Cam muttered.

"I'll look for footprints, or anything the attacker might have dropped."

Cam suspected nothing would prove conclusive. Julie's attacker could have dropped his driver's license on the spot where she fell and claimed he did so during the workday.

Alexa walked next to Cameron, but she kept her distance so that her hand couldn't possibly brush his. She looked so poised and put together this morning, acting as if their kiss had never happened. If only he could forget it.

Outside, the house hummed with construction activity. The hot-tub decking was finished and water trickled into it from a hose that must have been run from the main line. The sheriff took Julie's elbow and Cam reached over to guide Alexa around a mud puddle. Beneath his fingers, her muscles tensed, but she didn't pull away.

They rounded the corner, walking around an assortment of construction vehicles and supplies, and almost rammed into the sheriff and Julie, who'd halted at the sight of a forklift operator lowering a dripping-wet Porta Potti back to the ground.

The forklift operator saw them, shut off the engine and jumped down. "She's all pumped out and good as new. I hosed her down, too."

The sheriff frowned. "Didn't you see the rope around it?"

"Sure did." The forklift operator scratched his head. "I figured it was full and needed pumping, but she's ready to go now."

"You figured that out—all by yourself?" the sheriff asked, his voice tinged with disgust.

The worker's face lit in a proud smile. "Yes, sir."

Stunned, Cam resorted to muttering. "Amazing. Simply amazing. The one man on the construction site who is efficient, who needn't be told what to do, just destroyed any evidence the sheriff might have found."

Alexa patted Cam's arm. "It's unlikely the sheriff would have found anything."

"What about fingerprints inside?" Julie asked, looking unhappy that there would be no clues to solving her attacker's identity.

The operator's face fell as he realized he'd made a mistake. "I used cleaning chemicals on the inside, too, Doc." He turned to the sheriff. "I'm sorry."

Not as sorry as Cameron. Damn. He'd been hoping for the impossible—a nice easy solution to the questions that nagged him. He wanted to believe that the incident with the bull had simply been a careless ranch hand forgetting to bar the paddock. He wanted a reliable ranch hand to come forward and admit that he'd accidently bumped into Julie in the dark, that her scream had scared the man into running away.

Cam's phone rang, interrupting his thoughts. Chase told him Keith's temperature had returned to normal and that Laura wanted to invite them all over for dinner to thank him. "Can I take a rain check?"

Chase laughed. "You just want to play house, or is it you want to play doctor with Alexa?"

"Very funny." Cameron snapped shut his phone, relieved his nephew had recovered, and silently cursed his brother for calling up images of Alexa that had kept him tossing and turning last night. That kiss couldn't have been as special as he remembered. Yet he had to watch himself to avoid brushing against and touching the delectable-smelling Alexa every chance he got.

The foursome walked around the house, and Chase's phone rang again, this time a real-estate secretary reminding him of his appointment in town with a realtor. As Cam confirmed his appointment to look at a medical building where he might set up his practice, Alexa seemed thoughtful.

She kept her tone casual. "Since Julie can stay with the kids, mind if I ride with you into town?"

"I might be all morning." He knew better than to think she wanted to spend time with him. She'd set her expression to convey that her request was nothing personal.

Meanwhile, the sheriff and Julie had left them behind. Cam had Alexa all to himself for the moment. He realized the only way to decide if that first kiss had been pure dynamite or an aberration of his irrational mind was a repeat performance. There was no sense wondering about it, tossing and turning all night, when he could so easily discover the truth.

But Alexa must have read the sudden flare of intent in his eyes. She stepped back, slipping a little in the mud. Cam caught her and drew her against his chest. She felt as if she belonged there. As he breathed in her incredible scent, he murmured into her ear, "You needn't keep slipping in the mud to get into my arms."

Alexa's eyes sparked with annoyance. "If you think I slipped so you would... Why, you insufferably conceited, no-good—"

Cameron brought his head down and his mouth covered hers, hungrily. Last time he'd kissed her, she'd been surprised. This time she was like a hissing kitten, all fury and unsheathed claws. For an instant she could have pushed away, kicked his shin, boxed his ears. Instead, she offered as good as she got, flooding him with the taste of mint and coffee, impatience and greed. The engine noise of the forklift faded, as did the steady hammering and sawing. His blood thrummed to Alexa's beat, pouring music into his soul. Her response, electric, exciting, erotic, pulled him deeper, fired him hotter than he wanted to go. Somewhere along the line, his little test backfired. He couldn't imagine falling asleep tonight without reliving it.

Their first kiss had had him off balance. So he'd kissed her again to prove the first one had been an aberration. To get her out of his system.

But two such stunning kisses in a row could be no accident. Passion sizzled between the two of them and Cam had no idea what to do about it. He needed to think. But how could he think when all he wanted to do was take her back into his arms?

What the hell was wrong with him? There could be nothing permanent between them. She was only here temporarily.

And there was nothing wrong with him. He was a man with needs and hopes and a future. He'd never felt more alive and he shoved his previous feelings of guilt at his attraction to Alexa from his mind. For now, for just this moment, he wanted to be free to explore the here and now.

After he finally pulled back, forced to breathe in oxygen, her blazing eyes locked on his. Clearly furious that she had reacted to him, she quivered like overstrung barbed wire ready to snap. That she couldn't control her fervor made the memory of the kiss all the sweeter.

Now that Cam had decided to treat his relationship with Alexa as temporary, he felt lighter. Sandra would never have expected Cam to live as a monk. He no longer felt that teasing or kissing Alexa was disrespectful of Sandra's memory. Sandra would have been the first person to tell him that life was for the living. And Cameron intended to enjoy Alexa's visit while she was here.

She wiped her mouth with the back of her hand and spit words at him as if she could wipe him away just as easily. "Are you insane? You can't keep grabbing and kissing me every time we're alone."

"Why not?" he drawled, finding that he liked making her cheeks color, liked teasing until she lost the chilly poise and the simmering passion beneath was exposed. "I like the way you kiss. And you can't deny that you were enjoying yourself."

"I wasn't!"

"Then why were you kissing me back so hard my lips are bruised?" He appreciated the way her nostrils flared and her backbone straightened.

"That's not the point. We can't...we shouldn't...we aren't right for one another."

He couldn't help savoring her embarrassment as he chipped away at Alexa's poise and she fought to find words. He couldn't stop teasing her. "That kiss felt mighty right to me."

"You idiot. I'm not talking about lust."

"Nothing wrong with a little lust." Cameron cupped her chin and smoothed her lip. "You're lipstick's smeared."

"And your ego's the size of the Rockies." In one of those lightning mood changes that fascinated him, Alexa stowed her hot anger and regained icy poise. She cocked her head to the side. "Take me to town, Doctor. I have some shopping to do. And then you can take me to lunch."

Cam eyed the frustration and fury warring in her eyes and recalled that she'd never returned his credit card. Idly, he wondered how much this kiss was going to cost him. He thrust his hands into his pockets to keep from pulling her back into his arms, deciding that whatever she spent, that kiss was worth it.

Because now he knew—the first kiss wasn't a figment of his imagination. The second one had been even better.

ALEXA TOOK ONE LOOK at Cameron's expression as he entered the hotel restaurant and realized lunch wouldn't be the peaceful meal she'd hoped. Nor would they have a rational discussion over the impulsive kisses that made her pulse leap with excitement as if she'd just discovered a new Monet. There was something different about Cameron, something light and boyish that made him tease her with a freedom that took her aback. But their talk would have to wait.

Cam, too, must have fought his way past the flashing bulbs of cameras, pushed his way around microphones shoved into his face by the press, to enter the relative haven of Highview's finest restaurant.

The custody battle between the Barrington family and the Colorado senator's son made great fodder for news-hungry paparazzi. And they'd come to Highview in force.

Cam wound his way past other diners, ignoring their curious stares, and tossed a copy of a tabloid newspaper onto the table. "Who do you think took this picture?"

Alexa saw a fuzzy black and white shot of a bull charging, its horns seemingly inches from her and the twins' terrified faces. The headline read No Bulls in Boston.

Alexa perused the story, a sick feeling in her gut

as she realized how much the exaggerated story could hurt Cameron in court. "Your cook, Ray Potter, is quoted heavily. He took no time in selling the story. Maybe he took the picture, too."

Cameron closed his eyes briefly and then opened them as he rubbed his forehead. "My attorney says this kind of publicity will hurt us at the custody hearing. If the judge believes my children aren't safe, I could lose them..."

At the painful thought, his voice broke, and Alexa reached for his hand and squeezed. She hated to add bad news on top of the sensationalized story, but he needed to know exactly what he was up against.

She kept her voice low so as not to be heard by other diners. "Do you realize my grandparents' corporation, Levenger Inc., owns the subsidiary that puts out this tabloid? They also own several television-news syndicates. I expect the story may wind up on the evening television news."

Cameron lifted his head and thrummed his fingers on the table. "Perhaps my father could get a gag order..."

"He can't."

Alexa looked up at Senator Sutton, who pulled out a chair and joined them without being asked. She'd been so focused on Cameron, she hadn't noticed the distinguished senator's approach. But as he looked her over, she saw that his gray eyes were clouded with worry and the notable broad shoulders beneath the designer jacket, slumped just a little.

Although they'd met briefly at Sandra's funeral, Cam made the introductions.

The Senator's eyes narrowed and she was glad

she'd taken extra time with her appearance before coming to the table. Since she knew the Senator was more likely interested in her motivation than the color scheme of her outfit, she readied herself for a confrontation.

"So you're the Barringtons' granddaughter." The Senator kept his voice civil, but a steely undertone warned her the outward charm hid a shrewd and possibly dangerous mind. "I heard you were…visiting."

She wasn't surprised he'd known she was staying with Cameron. Highview was a small town and a powerful man like the Senator would keep informed, especially since she'd moved in with Cam on Sutton land. Did he think his son was consorting with the enemy?

"She's also Sandra's cousin," Cam told him, defending her before she could do so herself.

But while Alexa appreciated his help, she didn't require it. Luckily she was accustomed to powerful men. Work often took her to the homes and the businesses of the successful and the wealthy. The Senator didn't intimidate her and she let him know it.

Alexa held out her hand and the Senator took it while he perused her unhurriedly. She'd bet not much got past the sharp-eyed man and hoped he recognized honesty when he heard it. Before he could object to her presence, she let him know which side she'd chosen.

"Sandra's dying request to me was to make sure that her children were raised differently than we were. After our parents all died together in a plane crash, my grandparents took us in. But we spent our time with nannies and later in boarding schools. Sandra didn't want that for the twins. I gave her my word. And I don't go back on my word.''

"Glad to hear it.''

Alexa suspected the Senator was merely reserving judgment. They ordered lunch before he resumed the conversation. "A gag order is out of the question. You ever hear of freedom of the press?''

"So what *can* you do to help?'' Alexa asked with a boldness that at first startled the man and then had him grinning.

The Senator's dark eyebrow arched. "She's—''

"Sassy.'' Cam opened his napkin and floated it over his lap.

The Senator's eyes narrowed speculatively on his son. "I was going to say audacious.''

From that teasing look in Cam's eyes, Alexa knew she'd better steer the conversation to safer topics. "I'll take that as a compliment.'' Alexa kept her tone poised, determined not to rise to Cam's baiting her. She'd already seen how much he enjoyed teasing her about her reaction to his kisses. But she couldn't go there. Not now. "Senator, answer my question, please. We've had other trouble that hasn't made the paper yet.''

Cam shook his head and turned the page. "Julie's encounter is right here on page two.''

Alexa shivered at the thought that someone was watching them so closely. "Ray'd already left before someone attacked Julie. Another traitor on the ranch?''

"You can't blame the men,'' the Senator said. "These rags offer a year's wages for a good story.''

"We could sue,'' Cam suggested.

Alexa shook her head. "That would create more publicity, and besides, your custody hearing is already on the court docket—long before a lawsuit can be filed, much less settled."

"She's right." The Senator leaned forward. "However, I'm doing background checks on everyone. And I've put extra security in place around the ranch."

"Thanks, Dad. Add Leo Harley to the list. He's applying for the job of cook." Cam looked thoughtful. "In the meantime, I'll put off opening my medical practice."

"That may not be a good idea," Alexa said, recalling her talk with her grandparents' attorney. "The court will want to see that you're productive and stable."

Cam's huge fingers clenched in frustration. "What good is being productive and stable if my family's in danger? Someone let loose a bull, and if you hadn't thought so quickly on your feet, the twins could have been hurt."

"We still don't know if that was an accident or not," Alexa reminded him.

"Look, I hate to accuse anyone without proof." The Senator sipped his water. "But your grandparents have the most to gain from the boys' injury— which would help them gain custody."

Alexa shook her head, her throat constricting. These were her grandparents they were discussing. The grandparents who had taken her in and raised her. Even if they had sent her off to boarding school and raised her with a series of nannies, they had mailed birthday and Christmas presents. Sent her and

Sandra on a world tour after she'd graduated from an exclusive art university in Paris. Not once had they raised their voices to her, spanked her or even scolded her. She couldn't imagine them concocting this horrible scheme.

"My grandparents may be ruthless in business, but they aren't murderers. And I don't believe they would endanger me."

Cam ignored the food the waitress delivered to the table. "Do your grandparents even know you're here?"

She shook her head.

The Senator gestured to the tabloid picture. "They do now. Have they called to ask if you're all right?"

They hadn't. "They may own a string of tabloids, but they don't read them." Even as she defended her grandparents, Alexa knew someone would have told them about the story. Why hadn't they called Cameron's house to check on her?

Doubts filled Alexa as Cameron drove his SUV and returned to the ranch. She couldn't help but admire the way Cameron didn't badger her with questions about her grandparents that she couldn't answer. She also liked the competent way Cameron drove, as if unaware of the press following them from town. He didn't speed or curse or in any way acknowledge their presence. Cam had the ability to compartmentalize his thoughts, focusing with intensity on one thing at a time. She wished she had that ability. Maybe then her thoughts wouldn't keep restlessly circling.

Exhausted from her busy morning of shopping and weary from thinking over the possibilities, she closed her eyes and listened to the country song on the radio station. Beside her, Cameron remained comfortably silent, having no need to fill the quiet time with idle chatter.

Drowsy but not asleep, Alexa noted the reporters' cars stopping at the guarded gate after Cameron turned onto Sutton land. Thankful for the ranch's vast acreage that provided a measure of privacy, she looked forward to newly installed plumbing and a hot shower, maybe a nap.

About five miles in, Cam drove onto the bridge and over the water-swollen river that irrigated the fertile valley, watering acres of grasses. Cattle grazed peacefully along the riverbanks under a cloudless blue sky.

Peace stole over Alexa. Suddenly the SUV lurched. The bridge exploded around them, under them. She screamed, lost the sound of her own voice in the roar.

Flames from the burning bridge engulfed the vehicle. And they were falling.

Plunging into the river.

The seat belt chewed into her shoulder as the SUV, no longer level, pitched forward and downward, spinning crazily.

Startled wide awake, reeling with confusion, Alexa braced her hands against the dash. Up became down. The truck fell and fell.

Her stomach cartwheeled. Her head banged the door.

Suffocating blackness engulfed her.

Chapter Five

Alexa opened her eyes to the fearsome sight of water cascading into the SUV at an alarming rate. Groggy, as if awakening from a drugged sleep, she fumbled for her seat belt and turned to Cameron.

Eyes closed, face pale beneath his tan, blood streaming down his forehead and over his cheek he looked lifeless. He didn't appear to be breathing.

"Cameron?"

By the time Alexa released her seat belt, the river water was as high as the dash. Unstable, the SUV suddenly rolled onto its side. Still strapped behind the wheel, Cameron keeled over and disappeared beneath the icy water.

Alexa fell on top of him.

Unconscious, Cam could breathe water into his lungs, drown within seconds. Without hesitation, Alexa ducked under the water. Reaching with her fingers, she wasted precious seconds searching for his seat belt.

The frigid water slowed her thinking. She used too much air before figuring out the SUV rested sideways and the release she searched for was straight down. Finally her numb fingers found the seat belt release and pressed.

She tried to jerk Cam upward. But the straps had caught him in a web. And her stiff fingers couldn't seem to unwrap him. If he wasn't already dead, he would drown unless she freed him soon.

Opening her eyes didn't help in the dark, swirling water. She couldn't see the straps against Cam's dark clothes, had to go by feel while her oxygen-starved lungs burned for air.

Finally she untangled the straps and he popped upward. Alexa surfaced to find the water up to her neck, the top of her head pressed to the passenger window which now faced the sky. Freedom looked so close.

Yet she had no way to open or break that window.

Grabbing Cam's head out of the water, she screamed in his face. "Cam, damn you! Don't die on me! Breathe! Damn it, breathe!"

Cam didn't flinch. She had no idea if he was breathing or even if he still had a pulse.

The water rose to her bottom lip. They had to get out. Fast.

Alexa tried to open the door above her head, but she had no leverage to lift the heavy door straight up. The only other option was to swim down to the driver's door and out from the underside of the SUV.

Oh, God! Every survival instinct she had made her want to claw upward, to daylight, to air. Yet, downward led to salvation.

She tried pushing Cam aside to reach the door beneath his feet. But there wasn't enough room to slip by. He was too big. And she'd never drag him out by herself. She couldn't do this alone.

She slapped Cam between the shoulder blades, hard. He choked, spit out water, opened his eyes.

Thank God. He was alive!

She eased his head back and tilted her own chin up, too, breathing awkwardly in the last few inches of air space, praying he could hear her. "We're in the river, Cam. We have to swim down to get out."

He dragged in air in huge rasps, didn't say a word.

"Cam. Listen to me. The driver's door is below your foot. Feel around with your shoe. Use your foot on the handle. Open the door."

Cam's face, what she could see of it, looked blank. Either he was gathering his strength and saving air to make an escape attempt or he was barely conscious. Alexa had no idea if Cam heard her or even understood her.

A long moment later, Cam slipped beneath the surface. She reached to tug him back. Missed.

Water rushed over her face. The last of the air trapped with them inside the vehicle vanished in a swirl of surging water.

They would go down fast now. If they didn't get out before the SUV struck bottom, they'd be sealed inside.

They would die in this icy darkness.

An odd rush of water churned by her feet. Hands gripped her ankles and pulled her down, down. She used every ounce of courage not to fight going deeper into the water, used her hands to push past the steering wheel, out of the vehicle.

Cam slid his hands up her body and somehow she

grabbed his hand. He'd found the strength to pull them out.

Now they needed air.

The light above seemed tauntingly close as her lungs turned to fire. Together, they kicked and kicked to the surface, Cam holding tight to her hand.

When her head cleared the water, Alexa sputtered and drew air into her aching lungs. Her energy spent, dizzy, light-headed and half-frozen, she gasped and swallowed water. She sank back beneath the surface, couldn't find the strength to swim.

Somehow Cam dragged her to shore, made her crawl the last few feet. They both lay on the river-bank too exhausted to move, grateful to be breathing.

It took ten or fifteen minutes for the adrenaline rush to recede, for her breathing to approach normal, for her to appreciate she was still alive. Long minutes passed before her thoughts cleared enough for her to open her eyes and look around.

Rolling onto her back, she gazed at where the bridge used to be. "We almost died."

Cam raised himself on an elbow, cleared his throat. "I never thought I'd thank a woman for screaming in my face. Are you okay?"

"Okay? I'm not okay. I'm scared, cold, wet and mad as hell." She turned onto her side, and despite the blood still trickling from the cut on his head, he smiled at her. She wanted to slap him. "What are you grinning at?"

He kneeled, opened his arms wide in invitation. "Most women would be crying in my arms right now."

She'd like nothing better than a comforting hug

but refused to give him the satisfaction. "You bumped your head and aren't thinking straight. This isn't funny. Someone tried to kill us."

He stood and helped her to her feet. "You're too feisty to kill."

She stomped her bare foot. Somewhere she'd lost her shoes. Water and mud splashed over both of them. "This is no time for jokes. Someone detonated an explosion as we drove over the bridge."

His eyes narrowed and he turned to look at the bridge. "You're sure?"

She looked at his head, examining the laceration and bruise around it. "You don't remember?"

"I was driving and the next thing I remember, we were in the water. You were shouting in my face, being bossy—"

"I'm not bossy."

"—and ordering me around, as usual."

"As usual?" She made a fist, restrained herself from socking him in the gut.

"I happen to like bossy women." His gray eyes turned smoky, a look she was beginning to recognize that happened only just before he kissed her. What was wrong with the man? They'd almost died. Now they were fighting. She looked like a wet fish, and he had this look in his eyes like he wanted to swallow her whole.

When his admiring gaze swept over her, Alexa looked down at herself. Her tailored blouse molded her breasts like a wet T-shirt, and even through her bra, her nipples puckered and peaked through. She tugged her shirt from her skin, but her effort to hide her physical reaction proved futile. The material resisted all her efforts to hang loosely.

That teasing tone roughened Cam's voice. "Why are you trying to hide? You have a lovely body."

"So do you. Do I undress you with my eyes?" she snapped, humiliated, annoyed and frustrated. He couldn't just pretend she looked normal. Oh, no. He had to go and call attention to the fact that she might as well be naked.

He reached out a hand to her. "You can't fault a man for looking at what's offered."

She slapped his hand away with more force than was necessary. "You idiot. I wasn't offering. I'm cold."

Cameron sighed and threaded his fingers through his hair, winced when he touched the swelling bruise on his forehead. "And I don't suppose you want me to warm you up?"

"Sure you can."

He arched an eyebrow and stepped forward.

She planted her palm on his chest, ignoring his hard muscles, ignoring his warmth. But she couldn't ignore the beat of his heart, fast and furious, against her hand. Yet she wasn't about to let him kiss her, because she didn't trust herself. Whatever was happening between them was happening way too fast. She was off-kilter, needed to think, wasn't about to succumb to the we-almost-died-so-let's-make-love rationalization. Not when she still often thought of Cam as Sandra's husband. "If you want to warm me up, buster, you can lend me your shirt."

"You're nothing but a little tease." His eyes narrowed in mock annoyance, but his lips curved upward. "And my shirt is just as wet as yours." Still, he unbuttoned his shirt and handed it to her.

At the sight of his bare chest, her mouth went dry. Bronzed skin dappled with water droplets emphasized lean muscles in a tantalizing display of light and shadow. And she was no longer thinking of him as anything but a man. A very attractive man. She'd always known that Cameron Sutton dwarfed those around him, just hadn't realized it wasn't his height alone that made him stand out with no hint of weakness. His muscular neck emerged from brawny shoulders and a barrellike chest lightly dusted with curly black hair tapered to a flat stomach.

Alexa struggled with his wet shirt, refusing to drool over him like some bimbo. So what if he had a body Michelangelo could have sculpted? So what if she ached to run her hands over him in appreciation as she would a fine piece of art? So what if her hormones had a life of their own?

Her hormones weren't in charge.

Her brain was.

The sound of hoofbeats drew her gaze to a nearby hill. A rider on horseback approached at a canter. She had no idea if he was friend or foe. But they had no weapons, no place to hide.

Cameron squinted into the sunlight. "That's Bodine. He's one of our regular summer hands."

The cowboy neared, his gaze shifting from the torn-up bridge to them. "I heard an explosion. Thought I saw a vehicle plunge into the river."

"That would have been us." Cam, revealed his gift for understatement. "I'd appreciate it if you could lend us your horse."

"That's not necessary," Alexa interrupted. Even she could see that Bodine wasn't keen on lending them his horse. The prematurely graying, salt-and-pepper bearded cowboy's face stiffened.

Cam ignored her protest. "I'll send back another mount for you."

"Okay, Doc."

Alexa looked at the horse and her stomach fluttered. "I can walk," she insisted, avoiding his gaze.

"It's seven miles back to the house." Cam removed the horse's saddle and set it on a boulder before turning back to the cowboy. "This should save some weight. I don't want to strain his back with us riding double."

The cowboy nodded.

"And in the meantime, don't let anyone near that bridge. The sheriff will need to examine it for evidence."

"Got it. I'll see if I can fix some kind of temporary road block—at least on this side."

Cam took the horse's reins and led the animal over to the boulder, mounting with ease, his tone casual. "Don't blame you for not wanting a swim. The water's kind of cold."

Bodine looked at the shivering Alexa and laced his hands together. "I'll boost you up."

"No, thanks."

"My horse is gentle, ma'am."

It wasn't the horse she was afraid of, but if the cowboy wanted to think so, she had no intention of correcting his mistaken impression. Letting him think she feared his horse was preferable to stating the truth.

Cameron held out his hand, gray eyes bright with amusement. "Come on, darling."

Flustered, she snapped at him. "I'm not your darling."

"Ma'am, there's nothing to it. All you've got to do is sit there and hold on."

The expensive European finishing school Alexa had attended had made sure she knew how to ride. She also knew how to entertain royalty and oversee several households. However, her etiquette teachers hadn't taught her how to cope with awkward situations like this one.

Cameron's voice teased her. "Come on, the horse won't bite you."

At his taunting tone, she spoke without thinking. "I'm not afraid of the damn horse."

"Then what's the problem, sweetheart?"

"I'm not your darling. I'm not your sweetheart. I have a name, and it's Alexa," she fumed.

It was as if he knew what effect sitting behind his huge expanse of bare back would do to scramble her senses. She didn't want to sit behind Cameron, put her arms around his waist, cradle him between her thighs, and right now, he must be guessing her reason.

"I'm afraid of heights," she lied, grabbing the first excuse she could think of, knowing it sounded lame. Cam reached down, encircled her wrist with one powerful hand and tugged. At the same time, Bodine boosted her up, and before she knew it, she was mounted behind Cam.

"Hold on, sugar."

She gritted her teeth, gingerly put her arms around him. "The name's Alexa."

"Whatever you say, kitten."

Realizing the more she protested, the more he'd tease, she clamped her lips together. Cameron urged the horse into an easy canter, and Alexa had to tighten her grip around him. Her arms barely encircled him and she had to lean closer to maintain her grip. Even through her wet clothing, she could feel his warmth seeping into her. Every step of the horse, every bounce, pressed her breasts against his back, brought her cheek sliding against bared flesh. And all the while her open thighs rubbed intimately against him.

She tried to pull back, but the horse's rhythm kept sliding her against him, his musky male scent engulfing her every breath. To distract herself, she looked around, but the cows, barbed-wire fences and fluttering butterflies couldn't hold her interest for long.

When Cam slowed the horse to a walk, she tried once again to wriggle away, gain just an inch or two of distance between them. But the horse's back, slick from their damp clothing made her efforts futile. One second later, she found herself plastered to Cam again, and the heat seeping into her hadn't just warmed her. Her stomach rippled with tiny waves of taut tension. Her breasts, sensitized from the friction, ached for more. Refusing to think about how her body reacted to his, she took the opportunity to talk.

"How well do you know Bodine?"

The Senator had dropped off copies of employment records of everyone who'd worked on the ranch. Although Cameron had reviewed them, he'd already told her that he'd found nothing suspicious. "Bodine works here during the summers. Has a small ranch of his own north of Highview that he works during his off-hours. He used to rodeo, but quit after he busted his leg."

"Was he ever in the military?"

"I'm not sure. Why?"

"Well, someone had to know how to detonate that explosion. And he was close by."

Cam guided the horse through a gate into another pasture. "What reason could *he* possibly have to want us dead?"

Frustrated, she shrugged, and her breasts moved against his back. "I don't know."

"Will you please stop doing that?"

"What?"

"Squirming."

"I'm not—"

"Woman, you're wrapped around me tighter than a blanket. Trust me. You breathe, I know it."

"Sorry." Embarrassed, Alexa released her hands from his waist. If he continued to walk the horse, she needn't hold on so tightly. But now that her arms weren't holding her against him, only her breasts rubbed his back, somehow drawing even more attention to the limited contact. "Why don't I walk for a while?"

"Barefooted?"

She'd forgotten her missing shoes. She thought it'd be nice if *he* volunteered to dismount and walk, but he didn't. She couldn't just keep sitting there, rubbing against him like a cat in heat. "Maybe if I sat in front it would be better."

He chuckled. "Not for me, darling. Just sit still and quit rubbing your sweet little body all over my—"

"Shut up. Just don't say another word."

"And you say you aren't bossy?"

ALEXA HAD NEVER BEEN so glad to reach her destination in her life. The long ride back had been sweet torture, leaving her in turn frustrated, angry and embarrassed. She wanted to sneak into the house in her still-damp clothes, take a hot shower and wash away the tension thrumming through her.

They rode up Cam's driveway, and an assortment of vehicles revealed that visitors awaited. With the pipe laid and ditch filled in, Alexa surmised that at least the plumbers had finished connecting the water. If the electrical hookups had been completed too, she could dismount, go upstairs and take that shower she'd been dreaming about.

Grateful to slide from the horse's back and free herself from the constant contact with Cameron, Alexa walked gingerly to the front porch, aching in muscles she hadn't known she had.

Cam dismounted, too, and passed the reins to a ranch hand. "Cool him down and give him extra feed, then ride over to the bridge with an extra mount for Bodine."

"Okay, Doc."

Alexa headed toward the house, head down, watching that her bare feet didn't step on any construction materials. When a shadow loomed over her, she jerked and looked up to see a young man with earnest green eyes and the hulk of a body builder assessing her progress.

He stepped down the stairs to greet her and held out his beefy hand, biceps bulging. "Hi. I'm Leo Harley. I'm here about the kitchen job."

Alexa shook the young man's hand as Cam joined them. "I'm Cameron Sutton. Julie said you can cook?"

"Yes, sir."

"Have you seen the kitchen?"

"When will the appliances be arriving?" Leo asked pleasantly, and Alexa thought him a vast improvement over the sour demeanor of Cameron's former employee.

"Daddy!"

"Daddy!"

The twins spotted Cameron through the open front door, and tiny legs pumping, they took flying leaps into his outstretched arms. Cameron caught Jason in one arm, Flynn in the other. Both boys plastered kisses on his cheek.

"You're wet," Flynn declared.

Jason eyed Alexa. "You're wet, too."

"And dirty."

"Out of the mouths of babes..." At the new voice with the clipped Boston accent, Alexa froze.

It couldn't possibly be... "Grandma?"

Mrs. Emily Barrington stepped onto the porch. Regal and thin, her white hair cut in a becoming fashion, the Boston society matriarch took one look at Alexa's disheveled appearance and frowned. "You look like a ragamuffin."

Jason giggled. "Lexi's a muffin?"

"Can't eat Lexi." Flynn smiled at Alexa.

"I'd like to try," Cameron muttered low enough for only Alexa to hear.

She had to restrain herself from kicking him. She'd barely regained control of her raging hormones, and the thought he'd just put in her head made her senses start swimming all over again.

The front door opened, and her grandfather, Dalton Barrington, his silver-handled ebony cane tapping, stepped onto the porch. He held his head and bony shoulders with a proud, aristocratic air. Alexa hadn't seen him in months, but her grandmother's white-haired husband looked exactly the same. Stern. Disapproving and in total control of every nuance of his tight-lipped expression.

Beside her, Cameron stiffened, and without looking at him, Alexa felt anger radiating off him in waves. No one shook hands. To give Cam credit, his arms were full with the twins. And Grandfather didn't budge an inch, his haughty demeanor and pale blue eyes condemning them.

Leo Harley looked from her grandparents to Cam and obviously sensed tension. "Perhaps we should do the interview at another time?"

Cam shifted Flynn to the ground, then Jason, but kept hold of their hands. "If you could take the boys to Julie, I'll be with you in a few minutes."

"Sure thing, Doc." Leo, eager to leave, helped the boys up the steps, then disappeared inside with them.

"And to what do I owe the pleasure?" Cam asked, walking up the steps onto the porch and towering over the Barringtons.

"We were worried about Alexa," her grandmother said in her cultured Boston accent.

For a moment, Alexa thought they'd come out of worry for her safety after reading about her close call with the bull. She started to join them, actually feeling warmed.

As if reading her mind, Cam shook his head and she hesitated in confusion.

One moment later, her grandfather flung a tabloid at Alexa's feet. "Consorting with the enemy?"

Alexa's heart iced over. She should have known their concern wasn't for her, but for their precious reputations, and wondered why the newest revelation hurt so much. Her grandparents were as cold as a Boston winter, unbending, unfeeling, so sure they knew what was best for her. She'd come to grips with what they were and what they weren't a long time ago, but she'd never stopped hoping for the affection and approval she'd craved all her life.

As children, she and Sandra had never been told they'd done a good job, never been told they were loved. They'd grown up under a string of nannies and had been shipped off to boarding school at the first opportunity. Summers, they'd spent at camps and finishing schools. The only warmth in the big old gusty mansion had been Sandra and Alexa's commitment to each other.

Her grandparents had taught them that well-bred young ladies only had their names in the paper when they married and when they died. To her grandparents, having one's name plastered across the front page of a tabloid was the equivalent of committing treason.

Alexa looked down at the paper to regroup, expecting to see the photo of herself and the twins. But this article in another rag was different. Much worse. In this paper the first kiss she and Cam had shared stared up at her from page one in living color. Who had taken the picture? And how had they gotten so close to the house without being noticed by one of the hands?

She couldn't resist scooping up the paper for a closer look. She looked so young and carefree, happy to be lost in the moment. Her eyes were shut, a dreamy look on her face. Cam held her tightly, his eyes open and fierce, hungry, like a warrior claiming his woman after a long campaign.

Their private moment had been printed for all the world to see. Alexa had to stiffen her knees to keep from staggering toward Cameron. As if sensing her need for comfort, he placed his hand over her shoulders and drew her to his side, barely glancing at the photo. His warmth and support gave her the strength to keep back the torrent of ugly emotions rushing through her, emotions as primitive and harsh as this wild land Cam lived in.

She wanted to scream and shout. Pitch a fit and insist they'd done nothing wrong. But she refused to give her grandparents the satisfaction of knowing how much they'd gotten to her.

Anger flooded her at the invasion of her privacy. That someone had watched their kiss was despicable. That someone had snapped the picture and sold it made her feel dirty. Her throat tight, she fought back tears.

"I'm not the enemy," Cam said softly to her

grandparents, an edge of steel underlying his polite tone. "I'm the father of your great-grandchildren. Let's all go inside and talk."

Her grandfather pointed his cane toward the house's interior. "We've seen the way you live. It isn't suitable."

Grandmother fingered the diamonds around her throat. "It's dangerous."

Rage swept away Alexa's sadness. "How would either of you know what's dangerous for children? Neither one of you has ever taken care of—"

Her grandfather slammed his cane into the front porch. "Young lady, don't you raise your voice to your grandmother."

Alexa sweetened her tone but didn't hold back her true feelings. "I'm a grown woman and will speak however I choose."

"That's enough. This man has poisoned you against us. Pack your bags. You will stay in town with us until after the trial."

Molten steel poured through Alexa's veins. "And if I don't, what are you going to do? Take my trust fund like you're trying to do with the twins?" Alexa couldn't stop the bitterness in her tone. She raised the newspaper for emphasis. "Did you plant this picture?"

Dalton Barrington's mouth dropped open in surprise. "How dare you accuse—"

"—I dare." Fury such as she'd never known spurred Alexa on. "You want to control Jason and Flynn's trust fund so badly I think you'd go to any extreme, even sending the paparazzi to do your dirty work."

"That's ridiculous."

"Is it?" Cam spoke softly, razor-sharp anger heating his words. "Someone just tried to kill us. Yet, you made it safely over the bridge. And the only *strangers* around here have the most to gain from our deaths."

"Oh, God." Her grandmother's shoulders slumped. Her voice dropped to a whisper. "Are you accusing us of murder?"

"Come on, dear." Her grandfather started to descend the steps, his head high and expression unrepentant. "I believe we've outstayed our welcome. We're leaving."

At last. Alexa couldn't wait to see their car depart. Right now, she didn't care if she ever saw them again. Despite all her churning emotions, she knew Cam had the most to lose from the bad publicity at the upcoming trial. A sickening feeling about what could happen after this current fiasco had her shaking. Even the fairest judge might question Cam's fitness as a father after seeing that kiss plastered across the paper. People would assume Cam was a playboy, an unfit father. A good lawyer could make it appear as if he was neglecting his children and cavorting with women. And after learning about the accidents, a judge might place the twins' safety above the need to stay with their father.

Cam sighed and shoved a hand through his hair. "As much as I'd like for you to leave, you're not going anywhere."

"And why is that, young man? Do you intend to hold us hostage?"

"Nothing that dramatic. The bridge is out. And

until it's repaired, you're stuck here with the rest of us.''

As Alexa realized the truth of Cameron's words, she swallowed a protest. The unfolding events were worse than a nightmare. Her grandparents living in the uncompleted house, scrutinizing everything they did, would give them ammunition in court.

One look into Cam's steely eyes told her he recognized the danger. But they had no choice.

''Surely there must be another way off the ranch.''

''Only by horseback.''

Clearly the elderly pair couldn't ride out. On numb legs, Alexa sank onto the porch steps. She'd come out here at her cousin's dying request to help Cam keep custody of the twins. But her actions had made the situation worse. Now her grandparents would be watching their every move. With a sigh, Alexa wondered what else could go wrong.

Chapter Six

"Don't worry." Cameron squeezed Alexa's shoulder. "I'll have the Senator put up your grandparents at his house." He looked Dalton Barrington right in the eye. "I'm sure you and your wife will be much more comfortable there."

Emily Barrington's face, pale to begin with, turned paler. "We're stuck in this godforsaken place?"

Cameron controlled his temper. The frail old lady looked as if she thought Indians might ride across the valley and scalp her at any second. "Unless you want to ride to town on horseback or swim, you're our guests here until we repair the bridge and the sheriff clears you."

Alexa cocked her head to the side, and he could have sworn he saw a hint of mischief in her eyes. "You think the sheriff will suspect them?"

She might not believe her grandparents capable of murder, but she wasn't above letting them know she'd taken his side, and her open support meant a lot to him. "After our accident, we could see for some distance and we appeared to be alone. That means a timer set off the detonation. I'm hoping there're prints on a piece of the bomb.''

Dalton snorted. ''A bomb? As if I would know how to set off such a mechanism.''

Cameron's eyes focused on the Barringtons' burly driver, who stood ready to help his charges back into the car. ''I'll bet your man there knows all about explosive devices. He has the look of ex-military about him.''

Alexa nodded. ''He doubles as a bodyguard.''

If anyone had even implied—never mind almost accused—someone in Cameron's family was capable of murder, he'd be ready for a fight. But Emily merely straightened her skirt and kept her protest lukewarm as if discussing which tea to serve her guests. ''Paul would never—''

''Hush, Emily,'' Dalton said. ''Don't give them any information. They'll just use it against us in court.'' Alexa's grandfather pointed his cane at Cameron. ''You'd better go spend the time you have remaining with your sons, young man, because I've hired the best attorneys.''

Alexa sighed. ''Too bad your motives aren't the best.''

''Alexa!'' Emily's face pinched into a frown. ''You should know better.''

''I heard Sandra's dying wishes. She wanted her boys raised by their father, not a series of uncaring nannies followed by boarding schools and summer camps. And I've come here to tell the judge her wishes.''

Dalton pointed to the tabloid picture with his cane.

"You think anyone will believe you after they see those pictures?"

"Of course they will—especially after I tell them who owns those trashy rags."

Alexa's expression didn't change, except for a shadow of pain hovering in the depths of her eyes. Despite her brave front, she couldn't take much more of this venom.

Cameron had had enough. "Perhaps you would care to wait on the porch while Alexa and I go inside and make arrangements for your stay at the Senator's house."

Without waiting for a reply, he ushered Alexa inside, away from the cold stares and harsh accusations. That Sandra and Alexa had become warm, loving women after growing up with those two ice cubes was no less than a miracle.

He swept her immediately into his arms and kissed her soundly.

He didn't pull back until the twins started clapping.

"Kissy. Kissy."

"Daddy likes Lexi."

"And Lexi likes Daddy."

Red-faced, Alexa scooped up Flynn, and Cam did the same with Jason. Leo and Julie looked on from the kitchen with interest. Julie didn't look happy and Cameron guessed she was thinking about how to explain his actions to the twins. It was one thing to think of Alexa as a temporary visitor; it was quite another when their actions affected his sons. Cam knew he had to re-evaluate, but now wasn't the time.

"Make a sandwich," Flynn demanded.

"I'm the big cheese," Jason declared.

Alexa looked puzzled and Cameron explained, "We're the bread. Think of a four-way hug."

The two adults hugged with the squirming and giggling kids between them. Jason tickled Flynn. Flynn tickled Cameron and Cameron tickled Alexa. The four of them ended up on the carpet in a playful mass of wrestling bodies.

When Cameron looked up, the darkness was gone from Alexa's eyes. The kitchen door was closed. And the two Barringtons stared in the windows from outside as if they were looking at animals in a zoo.

Eventually, Cameron made arrangements and sent the Barringtons on up to the Senator's house. Alexa took her hot shower. And he hired Leo Harley, which wasn't a tough decision after he tasted the meal the cook had prepared on the propane grill.

"Yummy." Jason smacked his lips, uncaring of the barbecue sauce dripping from his chin.

"Absolutely yummy," Julie agreed before turning to Cameron at the picnic table set up in the living room. "Can I borrow a horse? I really need to go to class tomorrow."

"No problem. I'll make arrangements for you to stable your mounts with the sheriff's horses. Perhaps Leo should go with you. After that attack the other night, I don't want you riding alone."

"Thanks, I appreciate it."

"The Senator hopes to have the bridge back in working order in another day or two. Apparently the explosion took out the planking, but most of the braces are sound."

"Did the sheriff find anything?" Alexa asked, digging into the ribs with as much enthusiasm as the twins.

"He found a timer right off. It was still blinking numbers on the underbelly of the bridge."

"Any prints?" Julie asked.

"Not so far, but he's hoping to trace the pieces back to where they were bought. And he tried to question the Barringtons by phone, but they refused to cooperate."

"Why not?" Leo asked, setting out a dish of baked beans with bacon and onions.

"They said they wanted to help, but needed their attorney present after the accusations we made."

Alexa licked sauce off her fingers like a dainty cat. "And their attorney will advise them to say nothing."

Shortly after dinner, Julie put the twins to bed and she and Leo left for town and her one night class at college. Alexa settled at the cleared kitchen table, poring over house plans. Under her administration, the contractor was working diligently. The house now boasted running water and electricity. Windows were done, the drywall was completed, and the kitchen cabinets were up.

But without the bridge, no work could continue. Workers from Highview couldn't return. Appliances, wall coverings, light fixtures and carpets couldn't be delivered.

Since the Barringtons' departure, Alexa hadn't spoken of them. But when a vehicle pulled into the front drive, she jerked, and he could read the despair in her eyes.

Alexa's shoulders relaxed, however, as the Senator's deep voice boomed out. "Anyone home?"

"Where would we go?" Cameron asked his father. "Pull up a chair, and I'll find you some coffee."

Alexa looked at the Senator with troubled eyes. "Are my grandparents causing you problems already?"

"Not the kind you think. Better fetch a cup for yourself and Alexa. The caffeine will help you brace yourselves."

"For what?" Alexa curled a lock of hair behind her ear, a frown drawing worry lines on her forehead.

The Senator had a look in his eyes that Cam recognized—worry, excitement and just perhaps a solution to their problems. A solution that would work but one that Cam might not necessarily like. "Those newspaper photographs could cause a lot of damage in court."

As a former attorney, no one knew that better than the Senator. His tone didn't condemn or accuse. He simply stated the facts as he saw them. But what was done was done.

Alexa sat at the kitchen table, poised and collected, seemingly unaware that Cameron's father was up to something.

While his father took his time to come to the point, Cam fixed the coffee. "There's nothing we can do about these pictures now."

"There is," his father said mildly, looking from Cam to Alexa with speculation in his eyes.

Alexa rolled up the plans, and Cam handed out mugs of coffee. "You think the papers might print retractions?"

Alexa cupped her hands around the mug. "Retractions won't change public opinion."

"Exactly."

"So what do we do?" Cameron asked. "We only
shared a kiss or two. We didn't rob a bank."

"I've had some experience with the press," the
Senator said, his voice even. "The problem is, once
the public sees you kissing a woman on the printed
page, they'll automatically assume there are lots of
other women. Those pictures as good as branded you
a playboy. And judges don't like to give playboys
custody of their children. They might even prefer
rich and stable great-grandparents. Especially if tomorrow there's a story about you and the nanny—"

"I've never kissed Julie!"

"That won't matter. We're not talking about the
truth here, we're talking about perceptions. Julie's
young. And pretty. While she lives at the dorm on
campus, sometimes she spends nights here. There're
enough facts to support innuendos. And modern pho-
tography can superimpose alien heads on human
bodies. They'll have no trouble faking pictures of
you with other women."

"I could move into town," Alexa volunteered.

The Senator shook his head. "It's too late for that.
The damage has already been done. Now we need to
put our own spin on it."

"What are you suggesting?" Cam asked, knowing
he'd just taken the bait his father had so skillfully
offered.

"I'm suggesting a marriage. Yours and Alexa's."

Eyes wide, face paling, Alexa sucked in air. Cameron felt as if he'd just been thrown off a bucking

bronco and landed on his head. "Marriage?" he repeated, logic telling him he must have heard wrong, but Alexa's stunned expression said otherwise.

His father nodded. "A marriage would solve a multitude of problems. The public impression can be changed with your whirlwind marriage. The judge will like that you are no longer a single dad trying to raise your babies alone. And who better to help you bring up the children than their aunt Lexi—the Barringtons' granddaughter."

"But...but..." Alexa was like a bird about to have her wings clipped.

"We barely know each other," Cam objected while letting the logic of his father's suggestion sift through his automatic protest against marrying again. It had been one thing to steal a few kisses and tell himself it could do no harm since Alexa's stay was temporary.

And while Alexa wasn't a stranger, he didn't know her well. But he did know her enough to realize it would be wrong to ask her to give up her career just to please the court and help him keep the twins.

The Senator scratched his chin and looked at the tabloid picture, a sparkle in his eyes and a hint of humor in his tone. "Doesn't look like you barely know each other to me. And it won't look that way to the public, either."

Cam couldn't believe his father was suggesting they marry to increase his chances of keeping the twins. But the Senator didn't often interfere in his grown sons' lives—not unless he thought he could help.

Cam also knew his father was capable of matchmaking if the occasion arose. Although the Senator had remained single since their mother had died so long ago, he stressed to all his sons that raising a family was one of the most satisfying experiences a man could know. And deep in his heart, Cam agreed. His years with Sandra had been busy, exciting, fulfilling.

But Alexa was a far different woman from Sandra. Kissing Sandra had been like sipping a smooth cognac, while Alexa's kisses reminded him of tequila straight up with a lick of salt and a bite of lime. Living with Sandra had been the comforting soft rain on a tin roof. Alexa was the lightning that struck during a spring storm. Sandra had centered her life around her family. Alexa had a life all her own.

Marrying Alexa would be like trying to tie down the wind. And yet, Cam couldn't discount his father's suggestion without thorough thinking. "You really believe we need to go to such extremes?"

The Senator leaned back in his chair, took a pipe out of his pocket and stuck it into his mouth without lighting it. "I don't know. The damage this article did to your case is immeasurable. Do you want to take even the slightest chance of losing the boys?"

"But marriage?" Cam spoke aloud even as he considered the advantages. He could claim he'd brought the twins to this unfinished house to build it for his bride. The story would have a romantic bent, and the house would no longer seem a dangerous place to raise children. And the judge would see a stable household, a family unit with two capable parents, not a single father with a busy medical practice.

The Senator turned to Alexa, his voice patient and

concerned, which seemed to baffle her almost as much as his outrageous suggestion. "There's no one special in your life right now, is there?"

Alexa cringed. "My job takes me all over the world. I couldn't possibly—"

"—take a leave of absence?" Cam looked at Alexa, wondering if she found the idea of marriage abhorrent or marriage to *him* abhorrent.

The Senator shoved back his chair and stood. "If you could decide tonight, we could have the wedding…this week."

"Why so soon?" Cam asked, once again startled by his father's suggestion.

"Since the Barringtons can't leave, they'll have to attend the nuptials. And I'll have pictures taken of not just the happy event but their seeming approval by being in attendance. We'll leak the story to the tabloids, and those pictures will go a long way toward canceling the damage." The Senator nodded to Alexa and squeezed Cam's shoulder. "Please, think it over. But don't think too long. Don't get up. I'll see myself out."

Neither Cam nor Alexa said a word as his father left. Alexa avoided his gaze and simply stared into her coffee cup. Cam couldn't tell what she was thinking, didn't know his *own* mind.

To him, marriage was a sacred vow between two people deeply in love. And while he'd come to like and admire Alexa, and he felt an attraction to her— okay, a great attraction—he didn't necessarily want to spend the rest of his life with her.

Her work took her to the glamorous corners of the world. She dealt in precious art. She flitted. She didn't put down roots. Asking her to stay on a ranch in Colorado would disrupt her life, take her away from friends. He had no right to ask her to make such a sacrifice on his behalf.

"My father just made a suggestion. We don't have to—"

"I promised Sandra."

"You didn't promise to marry her husband."

At his harsh words, Alexa straightened her shoulders, and her eyes blazed with the attitude that made her so attractive to him. "Those pictures are just as much my fault as yours. I'm partly responsible for this mess."

"Maybe. But you don't have to spend the rest of your life—"

"So we marry," Alexa said. "Big deal. Divorce is still legal, isn't it?"

Her attitude hit him like a punch to the gut. "You're saying we wouldn't have a real marriage?"

"For legal purposes we would."

"And what would that do to Flynn and Jason? They'll get to know you, love you, think of you as their mother. Then you'd up and leave."

What would her leaving do to *him*?

"And if my grandparents win, how much will it hurt the boys to lose their father?" Alexa countered, her tone hard, her chin set with determination. Yet her hands shook so much, she set down her coffee cup and proceeded to twist a napkin to shreds.

"What about your work?" Cameron asked.

"I'll put it on hold." She drummed those perfectly manicured nails on the table. "After all, I don't need to work. I'm marrying a doctor."

Cam almost laughed at her sarcasm. Just like Sandra, Alexa didn't need to work. She'd inherited a
trust fund larger than most lottery jackpots. She
didn't work because she needed money but because
she loved what she did. And if she quit, he suspected
she wouldn't be able to pick up right where she'd
left off when she decided to go back. Jobs like hers
were rare and openings didn't come up often.

He didn't want to ask her to make this sacrifice.
But he couldn't lose his boys.

Images of Alexa—protecting the twins from that
bull, her ease at taking a shower in a horse stall, her
screaming at him to wake up inside the SUV—all
gnawed at him. She was brave and vibrant and full
of life, and if she stayed here, would she wither, and
blame him?

Alexa reached across the table and took his hand
between hers. "I couldn't live with myself if I let
Sandra down. So call your father. Tell him we're
having a wedding."

Cam swallowed hard, knowing Sandra would have
wanted him to accept this courageous woman's pro-
posal. He felt a presence nudging him toward Alexa,
and a pure red flame of approval bathed him. He
gathered Alexa into his arms and kissed her forehead
with tenderness.

He would accept her generous offer and pay the
price of letting her go if need be. Whatever happened
between the two of them, he wouldn't forget her de-
cency.

Meanwhile he'd decided not to tell the twins about
the custody battle or his reason for marrying Alexa.
Why worry the boys?

FIVE DAYS LATER, the wedding had been arranged. Alexa slept soundly and awakened on her wedding day to the calm certainty she was doing the right thing. She stretched, looked out the window at the inviting green ripple of grasses and the luminous clear sky. She wondered how the Senator would arrange a wedding with the bridge out.

Her peaceful feeling changed at the sound of little feet thumping up the stairs. Her door opened and the twins bounded into the room, chubby cheeks flushed with exuberance, eyes sparkling with mischief.

"Lexi!"

"Wake up. Up. Up. Up!"

The boys crawled over her sleeping bag and cuddled like wriggling puppies. Alexa put an arm around each boy, surprised by how much she enjoyed their sweet-smelling wet kisses.

Flynn whispered into her ear. "Aunt Laura brought you a present."

"Shh." Jason put his hand to his brother's lips. "Aunt Laura said don't tell her about the dress."

Flynn rolled his eyes. "You just told her."

"Didn't."

"Did."

Alexa kissed each boy on the cheek, then tickled them out of the argument. "It'll be our secret."

At the sound of a knock on her door, she looked up. A blond woman walked into the room and smiled cheerfully at the twins. She carried a delicate white wedding gown beaded with tiny seed pearls, a pair of white satin heels and a wispy headpiece. "Who's keeping secrets?"

The boys giggled and spoke in unison. "We are."

"I'm Laura Sutton," the woman introduced herself. The dress was on a hanger and she hung it on the door, then scooped up Jason.

"Hi, Aunt Laura."

"She married Chase," Flynn explained to Alexa.

"They made our cousin Keith."

"And the baby."

Laura laughed and smoothed Jason's hair. "You'll have your hands full with these two tigers."

"Grrr." Flynn barred his teeth and growled. "I'm a tiger."

"Grrr, yourself. I'm a bigger tiger."

"And tigers need their milk and cereal to grow up to be big and strong," Laura told them. "Why don't you boys go down and ask Leo and Julie to fix breakfast?"

"Do tigers like waffles?" Flynn asked.

"I'm not sure, sweetie. Cody will know. Hold his hand when you go down the stairs. After you guys eat, Uncle Chase is taking you and Keith for a ride." The boys obeyed Laura and toddled out of the room. Laura then turned to Alexa with a dazzlingly sunny smile. "That should keep the kiddies out of our hair this morning. I think this dress will fit. Do you like it?"

Not only did she like the dress, she liked Laura's friendly smile, so different from the sophisticated women she knew. Laura had calluses on her palms, hair streaked by the sun—not peroxide—and a down-home confidence in herself that Alexa found fascinating.

Alexa smoothed her T-shirt and crossed the room to the dress. "It's beautiful, and I thank you for bringing it. But isn't it too dressy for what the Senator has planned?''

"Not a chance. The Senator never does things halfway, and he has all the equipment, since he throws big parties several times a year. Tents are already up. The silver is polished and the fine china is set. Guests are already arriving.''

"But the bridge is out." Alexa frowned. "Maybe it's because I haven't had my caffeine jolt to wake me up, but how can the Senator bring guests to the ranch?''

"Most people are riding in, either fording the river where it's shallow or going around the long way through the mountains." Laura took down the dress, removed the clear-plastic wrapping and handed the dress to Alexa. "Judge Stewart, an old family friend, has agreed to perform the ceremony.''

Alexa suddenly turned shy with this self-assured woman, who reverently stroked the wedding gown. Knowing instinctively that Laura was offering her own wedding gown sent warm, friendly feelings through her. "Since we're going to be sisters-in-law, I'd like you to be my matron of honor.''

Laura spun around, and her grin, already wide, brightened. "I was hoping you'd ask. I have this fabulously wicked dress that Chase hasn't seen yet...''

Obviously Laura and her husband, Chase, were very much in love. From the glow on Laura's cheeks and the impishness in her eyes, she was planning a seduction.

"But first we need to get you ready." Laura lifted up a canvas bag Alexa hadn't noticed before. A curling iron, a blow-dryer and other assorted items overflowed the top. Laura dug inside and removed an iron. "While you take a shower, I'll touch up the gown."

"What time's the wedding?" Alexa asked.

Laura shrugged. "I'm not sure, but everyone who is anyone within five counties will be here. The press has their own tent. The Governor's flying in and so is another Senator and possibly the head of the Department of Transportation."

"The Department of Transportation?"

"Don't worry. He eats barbecued ribs with his fingers and teeth the same way as everyone else." Laura took one look at Alexa and paused. "What's wrong, honey? The Senator said you work around important folk. You aren't going to let a few celebrities upset you on your wedding day, are you?"

Alexa took several deep breaths to steady her charged nerves. A long time ago she and Wyatt Smithee, the head of the Department of Transportation, had been friends, very good friends. When Alexa stepped into the hot shower, she leaned limply against the wall.

Wyatt had broken off their relationship when she'd told him she couldn't have children. Pain swam like a demon to the surface of her thoughts, and all the hot water in the world couldn't wash away the old inadequacies, ugly doubts and bitter regrets.

Before winning his cabinet seat, Wyatt had been the youngest congressman the people of Massachusetts had ever elected to office, and the dashing politician had swept a very young Alexa off to the glamorous parties and charity functions of Washington, D.C. The Barringtons had approved the match. All of Alexa's friends except Sandra were jealous, because everyone knew Wyatt Smithee would one day be elected to the White House.

And now he was coming to her wedding to watch her marry another man. She hadn't seen him since that terrible night when he'd cruelly told her that his career was more important to him than she was—and that career demanded a wife who could have children. And since Alexa's ovaries had been removed due to a severe infection, she couldn't ever bear children.

Since then, Wyatt had married a former Miss America and together they'd produced four children. Alexa wondered if the woman had had to present a certified document from her gynecologist before Wyatt proposed. Alexa supposed she should have been grateful to have learned of Wyatt's ruthless ambition before the wedding. After all, what woman with sense would want to be stuck with a man who saw her primarily as a breeding mare to further his career?

But Wyatt had done damage to her confidence. Since then, Alexa had never placed herself in a position where a man would ask her to settle down and raise a family. Instead, she'd made a good life for herself. She had a fascinating career, friends in almost every city in the world. And for the past eight years, she hadn't ever seriously considered staying in one place long enough to miss the family she could never have. Until Sandra had had the twins, Alexa didn't even know she liked children.

And within hours she would be a mother. If she was entering a real marriage, she would have told

Cameron up front about her inability to conceive. But these circumstances were far from normal. No matter how adorable she found the twins, she had no intention of staying at the ranch to play wife and mommy for more than a few months. There was no point in letting the twins think she was more than a temporary visitor in their lives—just a fond auntie.

And Cameron? Oh, God.

She tilted her head back and let the spray of water spatter her face and neck. Alexa would have to keep their lives on a friendly footing. No more stepping over the line. No more kisses, especially no more of those devastating kisses that made her forget she was in charge of her hormones and not the other way around.

She would think of their marriage as a temporary business agreement. He'd win custody of the children at the trial and then she'd be free to leave. Maybe she'd have to stick around another month or two just to make the marriage seem real...but then she'd be free again.

Free to miss Cameron's laughter. Free to miss his easy relationship with his father. Oh, how she envied his big, warm family. Since she'd been here, she'd met only Chase and the Senator, but she remembered Rafe's charm and Tyler's steady good cheer from Sandra's wedding. The Sutton men, all tall, dark-haired and gray-eyed, drew the ladies' attention wherever they went. But it was their affection for one another that Alexa found so appealing.

Alexa stepped from the shower, wrapped a towel around her body and another around her head like a turban. She cleaned a spot of condensation off the mirror and stared at herself, suddenly full of doubts. She didn't belong in a family where everyone knew everyone's business, where the men stuck together and the women acted liked sisters. Cam and the Senator hadn't told the others that the marriage was temporary. She hated deceiving such good people.

She couldn't go through with this farce of a wedding. It might have been easier if the Senator hadn't made such a huge production out of the ceremony. Then it wouldn't have seemed so real.

Alexa now knew that she would have been making a huge mistake if she'd married Wyatt Smithee. She'd long since gotten over the man, just not the reason he'd rejected her.

Deep down, she recognized that Cameron Sutton was not the shallow excuse for a man that Smithee was—and yet, that attraction to Cameron made marrying him seem so wrong. He deserved someone better, someone who would fit into ranch life and into his loving family with the ease that Alexa collected fine art.

A knock on the door caused Alexa to jump. Laura's voice scolded, "You're not getting cold feet, are you?"

Alexa opened the bathroom door. "I'm afraid so."

"Well, come sit." Laura gently led her to a chair and pushed Alexa into it. Then she removed the towel from her hair and started to rub her hair dry with it. "I was a nervous wreck on my wedding day. It's normal."

"How did you know you were doing the right thing?"

"I didn't. I don't believe any intelligent woman is ever sure."

"Then why did you go through with the wedding?"

"I might have had doubts, but I loved Chase, and I knew he loved me. That's really what counts, isn't it? Love gets you through the hard times and makes the good times great. You'll see. Cam is wonderful husband material, and he has the same great looks all the Suttons have—dreamy dark hair and smoky gray eyes." Laura flicked on the blow-dryer, effectively ending the conversation.

If love made a great marriage, Alexa and Cameron's would surely be a disaster. They didn't know each other well enough even to know what they had in common. Alexa didn't know if he liked to read the newspaper on Sunday afternoons or watch ball games. She didn't know his favorite color, his favorite dish or his birthday. She didn't even know his age.

When Cam poked his head in the doorway, Laura shut off the dryer and scolded him. "Cameron Sutton, it's bad luck to see your bride before the wedding ceremony."

He eyed Alexa's cleavage below the slipping towel. "She's not dressed yet."

"That's another reason you don't belong in here."

"I like her better...undressed."

"I'm sure you do."

"You're one to talk." He stepped in and swatted Laura lightly on the rear with a wrapped present. "I believe Keith was walking before his parents married."

Laura laughed, not the least bit insulted. "Chase and I were lucky to marry before the second baby came along."

Alexa listened to the easy camaraderie between them with envy, wishing she'd had a family that had allowed warmth and teasing and genuine feelings for one another. Even if the Suttons accepted her, she wouldn't fit in. Her proper Bostonian upbringing kept her separate.

Deep in thought, she'd lost track of their conversation, and then Cameron placed the wrapped box in her hands. "These were my mother's. I'd like you to have them."

Alexa opened the box and stared at a delicate diamond-and-sapphire choker set in platinum filigree.

Laura oohed and aahed. "It's gorgeous and will go great with the gown."

Baffled by the extravagant gift, Alexa held the necklace in her hand and admired it. She looked into Cameron's eyes for answers. Why would he give her a family heirloom when the marriage would be finished within months?

She was about to protest when his hands closed over hers. "The Senator wanted you to have it."

"The Senator gave me emeralds," Laura said with a dreamy smile. "And I think it's a lovely tradition."

"But—"

Cameron bent down and his lips covered hers, swallowing her protest. His kiss had the usual effect on Alexa. Fire flashed through her veins and she forgot Laura watching them with interest, forgot she didn't know this man, forgot she wouldn't be spending her wedding night in his arms. All she could think about was kissing him back—and that she'd hate herself forever if she chickened out and canceled the wedding.

Chapter Seven

"Go ahead. Open them all," Cameron insisted, looking handsome in a black tuxedo that accentuated his broad shoulders and long legs.

Alexa, dressed in a sundress while Laura made a few last-minute adjustments to the wedding gown, looked at the huge pile of wedding presents in astonishment. Prettily wrapped boxes covered the kitchen table, overflowed onto the floor and onto the back terrace.

"Where did they all come from?"

Free from baby-sitting duties since Chase had taken all the boys for a ride and had yet to return, Julie, a vision in a scrumptious gold strapless gown that set off her tan, opened a pad of paper. "Guests have been arriving all morning. The Senator sent the gifts over. After you open them, I'll record the names and addresses and note what's inside so you can send thank-you notes, and then Leo and Cody will take them back to the Senator's to put on display."

"You'll have to hurry," Laura said as she stitched closed a dart in the gown. "The Senator called and said we need to be there by four."

Alexa hadn't thought through all the implications of a wedding. People spending hard-earned money on gifts for a fake marriage didn't sit right with her. Feeling like a fraud, she hesitated, not wanting to accept the gifts. But she had no choice. Making a quick decision, she decided to open the gifts and thank everyone, but send the gifts back after the marriage ended. Meanwhile, she'd do what was expected of a bride.

Julie placed a box in her lap, neatly removed the card and made notations on her pad. "Try this one first. It's from Wyatt Smithee and his wife."

Laura must have seen Alexa's fingers shaking. She carefully put down her sewing and leaned over. "Here, let me help you."

Get a grip. It was only a gift, Alexa told herself. But the admonishment didn't calm her jittery nerves.

And Cameron was looking at her with concern. He leaned over and massaged her shoulders, his warm fingers digging into and soothing tense muscles. "Relax, sweetheart."

Alexa almost slapped away his hands and told him she wasn't his sweetheart. Just in time she realized this was her wedding day and how ridiculous she would look if she protested.

Instead, she leaned into Cam's strong hands. "Whatever you say, beefcake."

Laura chuckled. Julie looked annoyed and rolled her eyes. Both Leo and Bodine blushed. Each young man looked at Julie, and Alexa found it amusing to watch them vie for the oblivious young woman's attention who seemed to hide from them by sitting very close to Cameron.

Laura smoothed out the fancy wrapping paper, reached through the tissues and pulled out a ceramic tureen, hand-painted in the exuberant Tulavera style. "How lovely."

Alexa's stomach finally settled and she swiftly and efficiently opened chaffing dishes, hors d'oeuvre platters, silk cocktail napkins, silver-plated bottle openers, stemless hand-blown champagne glasses. A Saudi prince, a friend of the Senator's, had sent a remarkable collection of dinnerware, a set for twenty guests with each piece a different design and showcasing châteaux of the world and their gardens.

Her favorite gift was from Rafe Sutton, Cam's youngest brother. It was a framed watercolor by a local artist who had captured the spirit of a horse and its fluid speed. Against the background of Highview's snow-capped mountains, a magnificent roan stallion raced across a verdant valley. Head up, mane blowing in the wind, mighty hind quarters bunched for the next bounding leap, the animal epitomized independence, achievement and boldness.

Alexa lingered over the painting, reluctant to put it down. "It's gorgeous."

Cameron placed the painting over the fireplace, and Alexa opened the next box. Julie tapped her pencil. "I hope a card's inside. I couldn't find one attached to the box."

Her thoughts still on the painting, Alexa reached through more tissue paper and uncovered the head of a porcelain doll dressed in a wedding veil. Carefully, she unwrapped the doll's body, which wore full wedding attire. But something was horribly wrong.

The eyes had been chipped out. A hunting knife

poked out of the doll's chest. Red paint had been splattered over the doll's wedding dress.

Heart icing at the sight, Alexa couldn't speak. Laura gasped. Julie dropped her pad. Bodine and Cody, unaware of the problem, remained busy carrying the unwrapped gifts to the car.

"Cameron!" Alexa held up the doll so he could see it. She couldn't believe that someone had deliberately sent such a nasty thing wrapped as a wedding gift. What kind of sick mind was stalking her? As fear twisted through her, she straightened her spine, determined not to give in. It was only a doll with red paint splashed on it. She wouldn't get hysterical. She wouldn't overreact.

From across the room, she watched Cam's eyes narrow, his lips tighten and a muscle in his jaw work. "Put it down and don't touch anything else."

As if she would. Wild horses couldn't drag her into searching through the box.

Cam had no such compunction. Leaning over her, he plucked out a card between thumb and forefinger. Touching only the edges, he read a typed message aloud: "'Don't marry him.'"

"What's that supposed to mean?" Laura asked, looking from Alexa to Cameron for an explanation.

"Someone is trying to scare me away," Alexa said softly, fear spiking through her. But along with the fear came anger. How dare someone try to manipulate her? Curling her fingers tightly into her palms, she drew a deep breath and released it slowly. If someone meant to frighten her, the scheme had worked. But she refused to give in to the fear.

"But why?" Julie asked.

Cameron looked at Alexa. "Our marriage will help me to keep custody of the twins. Obviously the Barringtons don't like the idea."

Laura peered at the doll, resting atop the tissue in the box. "I don't know, Cam. That knife looks awfully familiar. I could swear it's Bodine's."

The foreman? Bodine's? Alexa recalled how the foreman had been near the bridge after the explosion. He'd also been around when that bull had gotten loose. But why would Bodine try to stop her marriage to Cameron? She'd never met the man before coming to the ranch. Did he have a motive he alone knew? Or could he be working for her grandparents?

"Bodine," Cam called out.

Bodine came inside, and Alexa couldn't read anything but honesty in his weather-lined face. "Yes, Doc?"

"Do you have a knife with a six-inch blade and a blue handle?"

"It's missing."

"You mean you lost it?"

"No, sir. I had it last night. Took it out to clean and left it on the night stand. This morning, it was gone."

Cameron motioned the man over to the box. "Is this your knife?"

"Sure looks like it." Bodine's lips drew into a frown. "But I didn't stab this doll. What would be the point?"

"Someone doesn't want Alexa to marry me."

Bodine shrugged. "Doc, I'll pack up my things and leave if you want, but it doesn't matter one whit to me who you marry."

Alexa watched Bodine's eyes carefully. He didn't wince or avoid Cameron's gaze. He just looked surprised. Sounded sincere. But he'd as good as admitted the knife was his. Alexa wondered if her grandparents could have bribed him. Later, she'd ask the sheriff to look into his bank account, his background.

She really had trouble believing her grandparents would go to such lengths as to hire the cowboy to frighten her, but she'd never have thought they'd take Cameron to court over the twins, either.

Laura's lips pursed in thought. "The doll must have been purchased somewhere."

"I don't know," Alexa eyed the material carefully. "It looks kind of old-fashioned."

"Maybe we can trace it." Laura stood and shook out the wedding gown she'd altered and glanced at her watch. "Alexa needs to change."

Cam turned to Alexa. "You still want to go through with this?"

"Of course." With the court hearing less than a week away, she realized the timing couldn't be better. Alexa looked at her nails, then back at Cam and shot him her best grin. "I just need one more coat of nail polish first."

NAIL POLISH? How could the woman think about nail polish after she'd just received a death threat? Cam had to admit she kept a cool head. Some women might have screamed or fainted, but Alexa was made of sterner stuff. He could almost see the cogs of her mind turning, first ordering herself to be calm, then sensibly going through alternatives, options and possibilities.

His brother Chase strode in with Keith and the twins. According to plan, they'd ridden to his brother's house, where Chase had bathed and dressed the boys, then he'd driven them back in his car so they'd stay clean.

Looking none the worse for wear in his own tuxedo, Chase said, "You owe me."

Cam smiled and reached for his wallet as his sons and Keith raced by him into the kitchen. "What'd they break this time?"

"I barely turned my back on them."

Cameron took out some cash. "How much?"

"You must have eyes in the back of your head."

Cameron took out all the cash he had.

Chase shook his head. "I don't know how you do it. They found my toolbox."

Cam turned toward a kitchen drawer, figuring the cash in his wallet wouldn't cover the damage. "I'll get my checkbook. What did they take apart?"

"My computer."

"Jason! Flynn! Get your butts in here!" Cam shouted. Not only had they caused damage, they could have electrocuted themselves.

Keith stayed in the kitchen while the twins skidded into the den, innocent looks on their faces. Jason eyed his father's black suit, black shirt, black tie. "You look pretty, Dad."

Flynn scrunched up his nose. "Men aren't pretty, they're hand...dom."

"Handsome. And don't try to distract me. What did I tell you guys about electrical appliances?"

"They shock."

"We were careful, Dad. We took the plug out of the wall."

Why didn't that news make him feel better? "Why did you destroy Chase's computer?"

"We didn't."

"Didn't."

Chase kneeled down to look his nephews in the eye. "My computer doesn't work when it's in ten pieces."

"We can put it back together, Uncle Chase."

"Maybe you can, but maybe you can't. And in the meantime, how can I work?"

Flynn took Chase's hand. "We'll help you work."

"Sorry, Uncle Chase." Jason added, his expression a mixture of sorrow and a plea for mercy. "We just wanted to see the inside."

"Look at those faces," Cam muttered. "They have this apology thing down pat."

"That's because they screw up so often. They'd make terrific actors. Maybe you should send them to Hollywood."

At Chase's words, Flynn's baby-blue eyes clouded with tears. "Don't send us away to the holly woods, Dad."

"We'll be good," Jason promised, his lower lip quivering.

"I can't afford to send you guys away." Cameron shuddered. Just the thought of his sons around all that expensive movie-production equipment was enough to give him nightmares. But he didn't think it would hurt them to be reminded that they could be punished for their actions.

Alexa, a vision of a wrathful bride, swept into the

room and scooped the boys into her arms. "No one is sending you two boys anywhere." She turned angry eyes on Cam and Chase. "How could you two even suggest sending these two angels—"

"Those two angels just disassembled my hard drive," Chase complained. "And they even got Keith to help them."

Cameron enjoyed the sparkle that had returned to Alexa's eyes. Her nostrils flared and her spine straightened as if she was getting ready to fight the enemy. Although she wore Laura's wedding dress, she didn't look virginal but sexy, and for a moment he imagined planting kisses along her bare shoulders and peeling down the zipper at her back.

Would she wear frothy lace undies beneath the gown? Or nothing at all?

At least the stabbed doll didn't appear to have her too worried. But he wouldn't take any chances. He intended to stay close by her side all day. And he suddenly realized what torture that would be, breathing in her scent, pretending they were the happy couple about to share a wedding night. Cam almost groaned aloud.

"And where were you?" Alexa asked his brother. "Weren't you supposed to be watching them?"

"Dad called. He needed…" Chase threw his hands into the air. "Never mind. If we don't hurry, you'll be late for the wedding. And Laura will never forgive me."

"A fate worse than death." Cam chuckled wickedly. "I'll bet ten bucks you haven't seen the dress she's wearing."

"And you weren't supposed to see this one until the ceremony," Alexa complained.

Cam picked up Flynn and slipped his free arm through Alexa's. "I'm not superstitious. Besides, I don't intend to let you out of my sight."

"I shouldn't have let Laura out of my sight, either." Chase's brow furled. "I suppose her dress is cut real low?"

"With a slit all the way up to there," Cam taunted, knowing the slit only came to Laura's knee, but he couldn't resist teasing Chase. "Don't worry. I thought she looked terrific."

"Keep your eyes on your own wife," Chase muttered as he picked up Keith and led them out the front door.

Behind his back, Cameron and Alexa exchanged grins. The twins high-fived, believing they'd gotten away without being punished, but Cam knew he would have to do something to contain their exuberant curiosity without stifling their creativity before they hurt themselves or created more havoc.

Perhaps Alexa would have a suggestion. That is, if she stuck around long enough after the wedding to make a difference in their lives. He supposed he should count his lucky stars that she was still willing to go through with his father's cockamamie plan and marry him after seeing that scary doll.

Her courage gave her the right to be an equal partner, and he had no business holding back evidence from her—even if it made her unhappy. Cam leaned back in the passenger seat, willing to let Chase drive. "The sheriff didn't get any prints off the bridge's detonation device. However, he did learn something interesting."

Alexa looked at him over the heads of the twins, who were on their best behavior after the stunt they'd pulled that morning. "What's up?"

"The sheriff said that an automatic timer had been set to blow up the bridge. And it went off too early."

"That would mean..."

"It means we should have been way over the bridge and safe before the explosion."

"So now you think the scheme was meant to scare us, nothing else?"

"It's possible."

"And you think my grandparents—"

"Or someone they hired."

"—could be trying to frighten me away from you?" Alexa reached over and took Cam's hand. "Well, I don't scare easy."

Chase adjusted the rearview mirror. "Hey, you all. This is your wedding day. You two should be cuddled up and smooching in the back seat—"

"And mess up my makeup? I don't think so."

"—instead of talking about plots and schemes and—"

Cam grinned. "I wouldn't want to mess up her makeup."

"Of course not," Chase said in a tone that clearly indicated he thought Cam was crazy.

"Or her hair," Flynn piped up.

"Lexi's pretty," Jason agreed.

"She smells good."

"And clean."

Alexa smiled at the boys. "I do believe those are the nicest compliments I've received all day."

Chase shook his head. "You better hurry up and marry her before your sons get too much older and give you some competition."

Cam snorted. "Just remember you volunteered to watch these little guys for us tonight."

"Was I drinking when I offered?" Chase muttered.

Alexa turned to Cameron, her eyes full of worry. "Chase, can we take a rain check on the baby-sitting offer? With everything that's happened, I'd prefer to keep a very close eye on the twins."

"We'll be good, Aunt Lexi," Flynn promised.

Alexa smoothed a stray lock of hair off his forehead. "I know, sweetie. But I'd like my new family all under one roof tonight. That way I won't have to worry about you two boys."

Alexa seemed so poised and logical, it was as if she got married every day of the week. Cam decided she needed more color in her cheeks.

He caught Alexa's gaze. "We'll all stay together, but the only one I want you worrying about tonight is me."

ALEXA KNEW CAM was teasing her, but thoughts of their wedding night made her uncomfortable. Luckily the view distracted her. Chase drove past a ridge and made a gradual ascent to the north, passing a brow of massive cliffs and heading into the rolling valley where the Senator had built his home.

The house, although large, was not imposing on the land but blended into it. The design possessed a natural grace, a flowing grandeur that matched the vast lands and towering mountains that surrounded it. Solid stone walls, large picture windows with stunning views of the spectacular scenery lent an elegance to a house that the Senator could leave as an enduring monument to the future.

A long drive swept around an elegant curve that brought visitors beneath arching boughs of transplanted oaks, reminiscent of the Old South. As they rounded the house, the backyard spread out before them, a genteel setting of sweeping white canopies over tables spread with elegant white linen and crystal vases of lilies. A string quartet played softly and uniformed waiters served champagne to well-dressed guests.

As soon as their vehicle pulled to a stop, the Senator, looking completely at ease, opened the door and greeted them. "Right on time."

"That's because I didn't let the boys do a tune-up on my car," Chase mumbled, his gaze searching the crowd for his wife.

"Laura's making final arrangements with Judge Stewart about the ceremony." As Chase and Keith departed, the Senator took Alexa's hand. "I don't want you to worry about a thing. We have a boat ferrying people across the river. Security's very tight."

Alexa took in such subtle touches as the petals floating in a fountain, the ruby-red roses lacing the trellis and the lilac bouquet the Senator handed her. All the Suttons had gone out of their way to welcome her into this family, and the warmth almost overwhelmed her. "Thank you for arranging everything.

I can't believe you managed all this on such short notice.''

Julie walked over with Leo at her elbow. The young man looked about to burst with pride as he practically drooled over the blond baby-sitter.

Julie knelt and hugged Jason and Flynn. ''You boys look so handsome.'' She straightened their ties and then took each twin by the hand. ''I'll keep track of them until the ceremony. Laura thought you'd want them with you later up in front.''

''Absolutely.'' Cam touched Jason's head. ''You two had best behave or you won't get any wedding cake.''

''You look terrific.'' Julie gazed at Cameron and Alexa, and tears rolled down her cheeks. ''I'm sorry. Weddings always make me cry.'' Julie's emotion seemed out of proportion to the circumstances and Alexa wondered if Julie could have a crush on Cameron. She recalled Julie clutching Cam so tightly after the incident at the portable toilet, how she sat too close to Cam just a while ago. Maybe that's why Julie never looked at either Cody or Leo the way they looked at her. But then maybe Julie was just sentimental. She wiped her face with a tissue.

Leo took out a hanky and dabbed at her eyes. ''There now. You'll be fine. Let's go find the twins some cheese and crackers.''

Alexa caught sight of Wyatt Smithee approaching and took a moment to regroup. Pride made her stiffen her spine. She didn't want to let on that her marriage to Cameron was anything but the happiest of love matches. So when she turned to face Wyatt, she made sure that she leaned into Cameron and that she wore a polite smile.

Wyatt ignored her hand and gave Alexa a hug. "Congratulations, my dear."

In a fake tone and with a lack of warmth in his eyes, her former flame turned to shake Cameron's hand, and Alexa realized she no longer felt anything for Wyatt Smithee, not regret, not even a pang of lust, not even anger at the hurtful things he'd once said to her. She only felt lucky that she'd gotten on with her life without him.

Wyatt moved away, and Alexa noted that he'd apparently left his wife in Washington, which freed him to eye Julie, but the young woman was busy with the twins and Leo. So Wyatt's gaze swung to the stunning redhead talking to Rafe Sutton.

Alexa wanted to thank Chase's younger brother in person for the fabulous painting, but her grandparents approached. Rafe suddenly slipped away from the redhead, joined Tyler, the eldest Sutton brother, and came their way. As if by unspoken agreement, Chase and Laura joined them, too, Chase's eyes both fascinated and disapproving of his wife's low-cut gown. And Alexa realized the entire Sutton family had surrounded her. To protect her from her grandparents?

A photographer took pictures to record the event, and Alexa wondered how anyone would believe the Barringtons were happy about the wedding. Dressed for the occasion, but looking as if she'd just swallowed a pickled prune, her grandmother greeted her coldly and with disapproval. "Alexa, I hope this is what you truly want."

"It is not," her grandfather pontificated. "She couldn't possibly want to live—"

"Careful, Grandfather," Alexa said. "You wouldn't want to insult everyone, would you?"

Before he could answer or make a scene, Cam drew Alexa away, his arm around her waist, his hand possessively on her hip. "We're about ready to begin."

His brothers, father and sister-in-law closed in around their backs, physically separating Alexa from any further Barrington disapproval. Together, the family approached the arched latticework, Laura slipping into place next to Alexa as matron of honor. Rafe lifted Flynn into his arms, Chase held his son, Keith, and Tyler took Jason.

Judge Stewart, in his rich tones, began to speak of marriage. And the crowd of guests settled into silence.

Alexa's thoughts wandered. As her gaze glanced from face to face, she realized she wasn't just marrying a man, but was becoming part of a family. And what a family. These Suttons were strong, and they showed a united front to the world. The Senator, his four sons, daughter-in-law and the grandchildren all included Alexa without question, accepted her because Cam wanted them to and had made her feel more welcome than she could ever remember.

As she looked into Cameron's warm gray eyes, she realized how much she'd missed by always being an outsider, always being alone. Her grandparents had made sure she had clothes, food and a roof over her head, but they had never known how to give her the affection she'd craved. If not for Sandra, her childhood would have been completely barren of warmth and understanding and love. And if not for her promise to Sandra, she would not be here now.

She couldn't help thinking that Sandra was watching the ceremony, smiling in approval, pleased that Alexa would look out for the family she loved and ensure her last wishes were carried out. Alexa's heart contracted, and as Cameron slipped a wedding ring onto her finger, the weight of grief lifted from her heart.

She'd lost her cousin and best friend, but she'd gained an entire family. And when Cameron's lips closed over hers and his warmth seeped into her, she flung her arms around his neck and kissed him back with enthusiasm.

Then laughter and warm wishes surrounded them, and the twins' kisses made her heart melt with delight. For a moment, the joy seemed so real Alexa wanted to grab onto the dream and believe there would be a happily-ever-after.

The soft click of the photographer's cameras reminded Alexa of her ulterior motive for the occasion. The Senator needed these pictures to counteract Cameron's playboy image. And her grandparents had to be seen looking on with approval.

Laughing, Alexa grabbed Cameron and posed him beside the Barringtons for a more formal shot. ''Please, Grandmother, Grandfather. Try to look happy. It's my wedding day.''

The flashbulb popped and then Cameron swung her onto the dance floor. She swayed against him, her feet barely moving, just content to live in the moment, to enjoy the music and Cam's strong arms around her.

Because she feared the good times wouldn't last long.

Chapter Eight

Faces smeared with wedding cake, the exhausted twins slept in Cameron and Alexa's arms as the newlyweds carried them upstairs to their beds. While Cam tucked the boys in, Alexa dampened a washcloth with warm water and gently wiped their faces.

"They were good little boys today, don't you think?" Alexa asked Cameron.

"If you don't count the pizza they threw into the goldfish fountain."

"They thought the fish were hungry."

"And if you don't count their looking up their great-grandmother's dress."

"They only wanted to see if she had a rod up her spine." Alexa grinned. "They must have overheard some adults talking."

Cam threaded his fingers through his hair and escorted Alexa into the hallway. "How about a drink?"

"Sure." She turned toward her room. "I'm going to slip into something more comfortable—and don't take that the wrong way. As much as I adore four-inch heels, after dancing all day, my feet hurt."

Ten minutes later, Alexa, wearing slacks and a casual shirt, joined Cameron downstairs. He'd stoked the fireplace with logs, and the kindling blazed, crackled and snapped. He'd dimmed the lights and soft music played on the stereo.

But the scene was casual, not set for seduction. Leo and Julie worked quietly in the kitchen, putting leftovers into the almost new refrigerator—a temporary gift from the Senator until the new one he'd ordered could be delivered. And two security guards hired by Cameron patrolled outside.

Cam spread a blanket over the rug before the fireplace and patted the spot next to him. With a sigh, Alexa accepted the glass of white wine he handed her, the same wine she'd been drinking all day. She wriggled her bare toes and winced.

Cam noticed and took her foot into his warm hands. "Let me see."

He rubbed the arch and she started to pull back. "I don't think—"

"Yes?"

"—that you should stop that for at least another hour." She plumped a pillow behind her head, sipped her wine and sighed as his fingers did magical things to her tortured arches. "Your family's wonderful."

"Mm?"

"Whenever one of the townspeople asked you a medical question, your brothers and father saw to it that I wasn't left alone for a second."

"My family's one of the reasons I brought the boys back here."

"And the other reasons?"

"I needed to get away. But I thought the boys would feel more normal out here."

Julie and Leo finished up in the kitchen and headed for the front door. Julie's gaze lingered on Cameron just a moment too long, as if she wanted to say something and then changed her mind. Leo waved, his arm around Julie's waist. "See you tomorrow, Doc. Have a good night."

"It was a wonderful wedding," Julie added.

"Thanks for helping out," Cameron told them as the young pair left.

Alexa thought they seemed anxious to be alone together. At least Leo did. His crush on Julie was so obvious Alexa couldn't understand how the babysitter seemed so oblivious to him. But perhaps she preferred Cody. Or Cameron. Well, if the girl had a crush on her employer, she'd just have to get over it. Whenever Julie made up her mind to settle down, she'd have no trouble attracting a mate. But Alexa didn't dwell on her impressions of Cameron's hired help.

She sipped her wine, enjoying the first private moments she'd had with Cameron all day. She still had trouble remembering that they were married, that he was her husband. But she was starting to learn little things about him. His patience astounded her. She'd known he was trying to tell her something, and yet he waited for her full attention before resuming the conversation.

After she heard Julie and Leo's horses head toward town, she gave him the opening he needed. "You're worried about the boys?"

"My sons aren't normal." Cam's voice sounded

tight, and his fingers moved from her sole to the small bones of her ankle.

Alexa fought off the sleepiness that threatened to overtake her. Although it had been a long day, she didn't want to fall asleep just when Cameron seemed ready to open up to her. Not that he closed her out. One of those men so comfortable with themselves that they always appeared content, he rarely seemed to need anyone.

Alexa shifted to look into his frowning face. "I'm certainly no expert, but the twins seem fine to me. Their verbal skills are way ahead of their age group."

"Every measurable skill is way ahead of normal. Intelligence, sensitivity, curiosity, propensity for trouble, they're all off the charts. But they *are* bundles of high energy and difficult to control." Cam sat up and his hands slid to her calf. "I don't want you to think they're your responsibility. I intend to keep Julie around to help out."

"That's fine with me." Cameron seemed relieved by her response. She suspected he didn't want the boys to become so attached to Alexa that after she left for good, their lives would be disrupted. "This way I'll have time to finish decorating the house."

"And I'll be free to arrange financing and deal with the real-estate agent for my office in town." She must have looked surprised, because he explained, "A perfect building just came on the market. It'll need renovations before I can set up my practice, so I won't be abandoning you just yet. If I have to go into town, I'll make sure one of my brothers or a security team is nearby."

At the mention of the security team, her sleepy thoughts turned to her problems. The wedding had gone off without a hitch. No one had said or done anything suspicious, but she'd felt as if she was being watched. She'd tried to put off the feeling with logic. Who didn't watch a bride at her wedding? But the nagging feeling that something was wrong wouldn't go away.

Someone had tried to warn her off marrying Cameron. Now that she had, would the threats disappear? Or would worse things begin to happen? Somehow, as sleepiness pulled at her, her problems didn't seem that urgent.

Alexa twirled her glass between her fingers, fighting to keep her eyes open. "Did the sheriff find any proof that my grandparents paid Bodine to scare me with the doll?"

Cam shifted to her other foot and began rubbing the aching arch. "Not yet. And he says Ray Potter, my old cook, has left town. But something just doesn't sit right with me."

"What?" So he felt it, too. She wasn't surprised. Cameron wasn't only bright, he was very aware of what happened around him.

"Bodine's not the smartest cowboy I've ever met, but he's far from stupid. I don't believe if he were on the Barrington payroll, he'd be dumb enough to use his own knife."

Stifling a yawn, she sipped her wine and watched the fire flare. Cam hadn't drunk even a third of his wine, while she'd almost finished hers. If he intended to make her tipsy to steal a few kisses, it wouldn't work. She was too sleepy. "So you think someone stole the knife and tried to make Bodine look guilty?''

"It makes sense."

"Or maybe he didn't expect anyone to recognize his knife. How well do you know the man?''

"We hire him on as an extra foreman every summer. After putting in a full shift here, he goes home to work his own place on weekends and evenings.''

Alexa was having trouble remembering her thoughts. "I think…I think we should go take a look at his place. Maybe we'll learn something.''

Cam's eyes suddenly narrowed and he cocked his head. "Did you hear that?''

"It's probably the security guards that the Senator hired to make the rounds.''

"Maybe."

The logs crackled in the fireplace. The muted glow reflected off the planes and hollows of Cameron's face. He placed Alexa's foot gently on the floor, raised a finger to his lips and stood, then motioned her to stay still.

Was that a thud she heard? To her it sounded as if the noise had come from the pool area. But as moonlight filtered through the high windows, she could see Cam headed up the stairs, his hand gliding over the banister.

Confused and sleepy, she fought to push to her feet. She couldn't fall asleep while she was upright, could she?

Alexa heard the sound of cracking wood. Saw the banister give way and Cam stumbled. He broke his fall with one hand, flipped around and, catlike, landed on his feet while the banister came down around him.

Alexa started to hurry to him. "Are you all right?"

"Stay there." Cameron leaped over the pieces of railing and dashed upstairs.

Instead of following him, Alexa walked as if in a dreamlike state to the sliding glass doors by the pool deck. Without hesitation, she flipped on the deck lights.

At first she saw only the two security guards the Suttons had hired. But they were walking oddly, arms in front as if carrying heavy objects. As she peered through the window, the guards looked at the overhead lights with surprise.

From upstairs, Cam yelled down to her, his voice full of anger and fear. "Alexa, the kids are gone! Call—"

"The security guards have them! By the pool."

Alexa didn't wait for Cam to come back down the stairs. Grabbing the fireplace poker, she raced outside, trying to think how to delay the guards. Her brain seemed sluggish. But she had to think. She knew that both guards carried guns and that their arms were occupied holding the kids. But if she or Cam threatened them, the guards could drop and hurt the sleeping kids, reach for their guns. Still she couldn't just let them take the children to their waiting vehicle.

"Stop!" she ordered. "Where're you going?"

Upstairs, she heard Cam swear. Out of the corner of her eye, she saw him coming through the window and down the same ladder the guards must have used to kidnap the children.

Horses with riders and flashlights suddenly swung around the house. What the hell was going on? Kidnappers?

God, no! Alexa couldn't let the guards reach either car. She had only seconds to act. Keeping the poker close to her side so the guards wouldn't notice it, she raced around the pool, planting herself in front of them so they faced her and had their backs to Cam, who was descending the ladder.

"Put those children down!" Alexa demanded, fear making her voice surprisingly strong and commanding.

"Lady, move aside. No one needs to get hurt."

The guards started to brush past her. Alexa took one look at the sleeping twins' faces and acted. She stomped one man's instep and swung the poker against the other's knee.

The man she kicked swore. The other sidestepped the poker and threw a child into the pool. Knowing Cam had to be right behind her, Alexa didn't hesitate. She dived in after the child, praying Cam could stop them from taking the other.

Icy water slapped her awake. The underwater pool lights weren't turned on, and she swam frantically, arms outstretched, kicking madly. She had to find him. Soon. Her lungs started to burn. She refused to resurface. He was here in this pool. Drowning.

Something brushed her leg. Alexa instinctively pulled back, then realized her mistake. Turning around, she reached out and felt hair, then a head. Grabbing the baby, she kicked for the surface, fighting the pull of her waterlogged clothes, ignoring her icy fingers and choking fear. Suppose she hadn't found him soon enough?

How long did it take for a child to drown? She didn't know. Unlike Alexa, the baby had been sleeping. He hadn't known to prepare by holding his breath before going underwater. He didn't know to keep his mouth closed.

Alexa broke the surface and dragged the child to the shallow end. Cam jumped into the pool to help her. The security guards were nowhere in sight, but a vehicle tore off down the road. And she saw Julie and Leo were holding the other sleeping twin.

Had the security guards turned into Julie and Leo? No, that couldn't be right. The guards had been men.

Too exhausted to think, too cold to move, Alexa had no idea what had happened, and now was not the time to ask. Cam took Jason from her and gently placed him on the pool deck.

The child's face looked bluish. And he was so still that ice speared Alexa's heart.

That Cameron was a doctor made Alexa feel only slightly better. She didn't know how to perform CPR on a child, didn't know if she could summon the energy if she did.

Without panic, Cam checked the boy's neck. "His heart's still beating."

Cam opened Jason's mouth, tilted back his head and with his own lips covered Jason's nose and mouth. He blew in air. "Come on, baby. Breathe."

Jason didn't move.

Cameron repeated his actions. Jason's little chest inflated and suddenly he coughed weakly. Cameron turned him onto his side so he wouldn't choke on the water. "It's okay, little guy. You'll be just fine."

Alexa still panted from her exertions, but she couldn't seem to move. As her adrenaline-induced strength faded, she started to shake and shiver. Drowsiness stole away any desire to pick herself up and move inside.

Beside her, Cameron wrapped a sleepy Jason in his shirt. "Alexa, are you hurt? Thanks to you, Jason will be just fine."

"What about b-brain d-damage?"

"He wasn't under long enough."

It had seemed like forever to her. "Maybe we should take him to the hospital—just to be sure."

"Luckily the sleeping drug they gave him is already wearing off. He'll be fine." Cameron looked at Alexa who could barely keep her eyes open. "I suspect you swallowed some of the sleeping drug, too." His gaze swung to Julie. "Is Flynn awake?"

"Barely." Julie, her voice tight with worry, smoothed back Flynn's black curls.

Leo led her with the baby through the sliding glass door. "We should get them out of the night air. It's chilly."

"Good idea." Cameron tucked Jason close to one broad shoulder and helped Alexa to her feet with his free hand.

"I don't feel very good."

"Don't fall asleep until I get you inside."

"I won't," Alexa promised, wondering if she would do just that. She felt so tired, her eyelids so heavy. Her eyes closed, her head flopped onto Cameron's shoulder, and boneless, she let him half-lead, half-carry her inside. The warmth from the fire wrapped around her like a blanket.

Somewhere in her mind, questions tried to form and make it out of her mouth. But she could no longer fight the sleepy darkness.

ALEXA AWAKENED in her room to the smell of bacon, strong coffee and hot cinnamon buns. Cameron had brought up a tray of breakfast for two, his eyes weary as if he hadn't slept all night—their wedding night. Her cloudy thoughts suddenly cleared and last night's events rushed back to her. "The boys?"

"Are fine. I stayed up all night just to be sure. And Jason's lungs are clear. He suffered no ill effects from the water."

Cameron set the tray on the floor by her sleeping bag. Alexa realized someone had removed her wet clothes, for she was naked beneath a blanket.

Cameron must have read the alarm in her eyes. "I carried you up here and helped Julie take off your shirt and slacks. She removed your wet underwear and covered you with the blanket."

Alexa didn't like the idea of anyone undressing her, but she'd been unconscious. Wrapping the blanket around her, she stood, picked up some clothing out of her open luggage and headed for the bathroom.

She returned fully dressed to find half the breakfast gone and Cameron swallowing coffee. She helped herself to a cinnamon bun and nibbled. "Could you fill me in on what happened last night? Between the sleeping drug and the time I spent underwater, I can't seem to make sense of it."

"The security guards tried to kidnap the twins."

She'd guessed that much. "Why?"

"I don't know. They're very wealthy little boys. Maybe someone wanted to ransom them back to us."

"Or maybe this was another attempt to make it appear as if you aren't a good father. Maybe the guards didn't intend to kidnap the boys, but only to make it appear you'd lost them for a while."

"Did you get a look at their faces?"

"It was too dark."

"What about their getaway car?" Cameron asked.

She shook her head, realizing the guards had escaped. "I was underwater, remember? I don't even know how Julie and Leo got there."

"Julie forgot her backpack with her schoolbooks. She had to study for a test, so they returned to pick it up."

Alexa recalled Leo's flashlights. "But they came around back."

"After you flipped on the porch lights, they saw the guards trying to take the children and rode straight to the backyard. Leo tried to catch the guards but he tripped, and both guards managed to slip away."

"Is the bridge still out?" Alexa asked, wondering where the guards had driven. She suspected they'd ditched the car in the woods and swum across the river in the dark.

"The bridge won't hold a car, but it's strong enough for horses. Why?"

"Your father hired the guards from a firm in town. It shouldn't be too hard to figure out who they are. and then press charges with the sheriff."

WITH TYLER GUARDING the house, Cameron and Alexa left the twins under Julie's watchful eye and rode out right after breakfast. Cameron wished he could have thought of a reason to ride with Alexa again, instead of letting her ride her own mount. Their last ride together had been incredibly sexy, and despite his worry about the upcoming custody hearing and the twins, he couldn't help noticing Alexa.

The big bay mare she rode could stick to a calf like a burr on a sheep's tail, but seemed to be enjoying a morning free from its usual work. The bay pranced and Alexa rode her with an easy expertise that revealed lots of riding lessons at expensive boarding schools back East.

Alexa tipped back the hat she'd insisted on borrowing to shield her face from the summer sun and took in the green pastures they rode through, with pleasure glinting in her eyes. "I can understand why your family has become so attached to this land."

"You should see the valley from up there." He pointed to the towering mountains that made a picture-perfect backdrop for the peaceful pastureland.

"I'd like to try and paint it."

"I didn't know you painted."

"I dabble in oils." She shrugged. "When I figured out I wasn't good enough to sell my work, I started selling other artists' work to galleries, collectors and museums."

During the ride to town, she told him several amusing stories about eccentric clients, picky museum directors and her search for the perfect Dali to hang over Donald Trump's sofa. Her voice rang with a vibrancy while her words conveyed her expertise.

The bottom line was that she clearly loved her work—work she couldn't do while she remained with him.

He reminded himself that their marriage was simply a convenient way for him to show the court he was stable. Nothing more than a piece of paper filed in a courthouse—and this paper gave him no right to think of Alexa in any special way. Yet, how could he not be affected by her sunny smile, her bright-eyed enthusiasm and her unflagging courage?

Once again last night she'd helped him save his boys. If she hadn't dived into the dark pool after Jason…he shuddered to think what might have happened. And she did it while drugged from some kind of sleeping tablet. Cameron had saved the remainder of her wine in a vial for the sheriff to send to be tested. And he'd wrapped the wine bottle carefully in newspaper, hoping someone had left fingerprints.

Cameron knew he owed Alexa more than he could ever repay her, and he had no right to try to convince her to stay with him and the boys. She clearly had her own life, where she was happy. It would be wrong to use the sexual attraction they felt for one another to try to change her mind about leaving. And yet, he couldn't seem to stop himself from dwelling on how he felt.

He found her too attractive. With her face pleasantly flushed from the ride, wisps of hair escaping from her braid and curling around her face, he wanted to take her up onto his horse and kiss her.

When they rode over the newly reconstructed and almost completed bridge, Cam was grateful for the distraction. Bodine had a crew of about thirty men hammering planks across the surface, a concrete truck pouring bases, while extra steel bracing had been added below. Assorted backhoes, loaders, paving equipment and rollers were working on different sections of road.

Cameron pulled up his horse to speak with his foreman. "Did any vehicles try to cross the bridge last night?"

"No, Doc." Bodine wiped the sweat off his brow. "If those security guards had tried to escape this way, they would have fallen into the river. We don't have all the braces in yet, but it'll hold your horses. If those men kept the car, they must have gone through the mountains."

"I didn't think that was possible," Alexa said.

"A four-wheel-drive could make it to town in an hour if they drove over the train tracks," Cameron answered.

Alexa shook her head. "Over the train tracks?"

"My brothers and I did it when we were young and—"

"—stupid?"

Cameron grinned and turned back to Bodine. "How long before you're finished?"

"I'm hoping we'll have it done today, sir."

"Good," Alexa murmured, shifting uncomfortably in her saddle. Clearly unaccustomed to riding for miles and miles, she would be sore later, and Cameron tried unsuccessfully to refrain from even thinking about rubbing her aching derriere. Alexa had terrific legs, smooth, lean, muscular. And his fingers itched to explore her ankles and calves and thighs. Just the thought of those legs brought erotic images of them wrapped around his waist.

Thoughts of what he'd like to do with her had his jeans tightening uncomfortably in places. To get his mind off making love to her, he urged his horse faster.

"Come on. Another hour and we'll make it to town. Last one there buys lunch."

IN SMALL TOWNS many businesses did double duty by performing two services. The local pharmacy rented bicycles to tourists, a weight loss clinic met at the health food store at night. The security agency in Highview doubled as a tourist center that offered guides. A poster on the door advertised white-water-rafting trips, four-wheel-drive vehicles for rent and camping expeditions.

As Alexa walked inside and her eyes adjusted to the dim interior, she saw mountain bikes, camping and fishing gear, wind sailing masts and boards stacked against the walls. And farther back were skis, boots and snowboards, along with the necessary clothing.

A salesclerk approached Cam with an appreciative smile that faded when she saw Alexa. "May I help you?"

"I'd like to speak to the manager, please."

"This way, sir." The clerk led them through a twisting aisle to the rear of the store. Cam took Alexa's hand in a proprietary gesture that arrowed heat up her arm and into her core. Alexa wanted to pull away, but knew if she did, it would be tantamount to admitting how much he affected her.

The clerk knocked twice on a door, then opened it. "Jess, there's some folks here who want to speak with you."

A tall, gray-haired woman with a muscular frame, peeked over her glasses at them. She gestured to two hard-backed chairs by her desk. "Please come in. What can I do for you?"

"I'm Cameron Sutton and this is...my wife Alexa." Jess may not have noticed the hesitation in Cam's voice, but Alexa had. Not that she blamed him. She had trouble remembering she was married herself. But she was especially glad that Cameron was no longer holding her hand. Now that she was free of his disturbingly evocative touch, she could regain control of her reactions.

"Jess Parker." The woman offered her hand to Cam, then Alexa. "What can I help you with?" she asked again.

"I'd like to see the employment records of the security guards my father hired from your firm."

"I'm sorry. Employment applications are confidential. Is there a problem?"

Cameron's eyes flashed gunmetal gray. "Two security guards tried to kidnap my children."

Jess Parker's jaw dropped open in horror. "What! You're serious? I just hired two new men because your father increased security and has temporarily hired every security guard that I could find. The new men's records are impeccable. And though they insisted on working as partners, I didn't suspect anything." Jess stood, walked to her file cabinet and pulled out two folders, which she handed to Cam.

"You can see they came with the best recommendations."

"Did you check these Denver references?" Alexa asked as she peered at the records while trying to ignore Cameron's spicy scent that mixed so well with leather.

"Yes, I did. We may not be a large operation, but we pride ourselves on our personnel. That's why the Senator uses my services. In all the years we've operated, nothing like this has ever happened. Are your children all right?"

"They're safe now." Cam read the applications and frowned, his bottom lip puckering, and Alexa had the sudden thought of nipping at it until he relaxed. "Stephen Rayes and James Philbin. They shared a residence. Ms. Parker, would you mind making copies of this address, their social security numbers and references for the sheriff?"

"Not at all. I'm very sorry you had trouble. You'll receive a full refund, of course. And if there's anything else I can do, please let me know."

Alexa forced her thoughts away from comforting Cam or distracting him with a series of kisses. "You wouldn't have any pictures of the men, would you?"

"Their pictures are on their security licenses, and a copy is attached to the back of each man's file."

Alexa's hopes soared. If they had pictures of the men, they could show them around town and ask questions. They could take the pictures to the police, banks and the phone company. It was a tremendous break to have pictures of the men who'd tried to abduct Cam's children.

Cameron turned over both files, his big hands sure and agile. Neither picture remained.

CAMERON AND ALEXA left their horses in the sheriff's stable, where Noel Demory picked them up. Cam handed the sheriff the bottle of wine he'd saved and the files. After noting the addresses in the files, the sheriff swung a right and headed east toward an apartment complex west of Highview.

Alexa wanted to go straight to the security guards' apartment, but the sheriff insisted they check in with the apartment manager first. And once again, Cameron took her hand as they walked toward the site's office. She wondered if he was deliberately trying to throw her off balance by this constant touching. Or was he just being polite? Surely holding her hand couldn't mean as little to him as it appeared or he wouldn't keep doing it.

Maybe he thought married couples, newlyweds, should always be touching. If so, she found the idea sweet, but she still wished he wouldn't. His touch made her think of him as a man, an attractive man who enjoyed her touch.

A curvy redhead with big hair and a surly smile greeted them in a tiny office. She shoved fingernail polish into a drawer and fanned her wet nails to air-dry.

"I'm looking for Stephen Rayes and James Philbin, ma'am," the sheriff said.

"They were in apartment 313."

"Were?" Cam asked, his voice even but edged with steel. His fingers tightened around Alexa's.

"Moved out in the middle of the night." The redhead looked at Alexa and Cameron. "They'd already paid up for the month. I can give you a deal if you want to move in…"

"I'd like to look at the apartment, please," Alexa said, hoping that maybe their suspects had left some clues, but it seemed as if the would-be kidnappers were two steps ahead of them. She could almost feel Cam's disappointment adding to her own.

The redhead dug out a key and the sheriff asked for the guards' apartment application. Alexa didn't see new clues on this form. Just the same information again.

While she, Cameron and the sheriff walked to the apartment, the sheriff called in the social-security numbers on the radio. A few minutes later, an officer called back. "Noel, the social-security numbers don't match the names. And Stephen Rayes is a seventy-four-year-old black male who reported his wallet stolen in Denver last month."

Cameron rubbed his brow with his free hand as he walked beside Alexa and spoke to Noel. "Does that mean the names were fake?"

"Yep. I'd be willing to bet the references don't check out, either, Doc."

Alexa sighed with disappointment. "So we have no idea who those two men really were."

"Or who may have hired them to kidnap the twins." Cam seemed thoughtful—and worried. And Alexa couldn't blame him. Whoever was after the twins could make another attempt. Until they figured out who was behind the scheme, they couldn't be sure of the twins' safety.

The sheriff put the key in the lock and opened the

front door. One look and Alexa's hopes vanished. The apartment was completely empty. The two kidnappers hadn't left behind so much as a dirty ashtray. Disappointment flooded her. All these questions, all the searching, and they seemed no closer to figuring out what was going on than before they started investigating. Frustrated, she turned to Cam, hugged him and looked into his steady gray eyes. "Now what?"

Chapter Nine

"We can check the phone numbers in Denver," Cam suggested, but Alexa could tell he wasn't hopeful. Still, with one arm came around her waist, he hugged her tightly for one breathless moment before releasing her.

Alexa sighed, missing his touch but glad he'd found a little comfort in her hug. "The phones are probably disconnected or bogus numbers."

Cam shook his head. "Maybe not. Jess Parker told us she called and checked the references. Someone vouched for those two men."

After calling officers to dust the apartment for fingerprints, the sheriff drove them back through town to the hotel, where they'd eat lunch. "Maybe we'll get lucky and they'll have paid the Denver phone bill by check." Noel wrote down Cameron's cell phone number and promised to let them know about the drugged wine, the fingerprints and the phone numbers as soon as he had any information.

After lunch, Cam borrowed a car from the real-estate agent who was selling him the medical building. He made a brief stop to check on the site, but soon pulled onto a road heading north out of town.

With a cocky set to his jaw, he tuned the radio. "I thought we'd pay Bodine a little visit."

"He isn't still working, is he?" Alexa asked, thinking back to the last time she'd seen the foreman that morning. He'd been busy overseeing the reconstruction of the bridge. Bodine had seemed determined to finish the job today.

But then, Colorado seemed filled with determined men, none more so than her husband. Despite their problems, he never lost an opportunity to brush against her, touch her hand, take her elbow, constantly reminding her that he found her attractive. She didn't believe he was acting to convince others their marriage was real. She could see the need simmering in his eyes, feel the tension radiating off him, knew that even a man with Cameron's patience couldn't hold back his passion forever.

But she had no idea what she wanted to do about it. She would be leaving soon after the trial. If she became any more attached to Cameron and the twins, leaving would be impossible. For just a little while, she could step into another woman's role and be a mother, a wife. This opportunity might never come again. Perhaps she should accept the invitation in Cameron's eyes and touch, and make the most of her time here. She could worry about paying the price after she was gone.

Cameron's husky voice interrupted her thoughts. "Bodine and his crew started at five this morning. They quit at three and that's a ten-hour day." Cameron checked his watch. "He should be home by now."

"See if you can work in a way to ask the man if he's ever been in the military or in mining," Alexa suggested, refocusing her thoughts on the problem with effort.

"Why?"

"Whoever blew up that bridge was familiar with explosives."

"Not necessarily. Remember the charge went off too soon?"

Cameron's patience to consider every detail annoyed her, but she couldn't fault his logic. He seemed so calm and methodical. Didn't he know how much his touches raised her pulse? Did he have any idea how much she enjoyed working with him? In all the years she'd known him, he'd never lost his temper, never raised his voice in anger. In fact, the only time he showed real emotion was when he played with his boys. And when he kissed her.

On the scale of one to ten, the man's kisses were a definite twelve. But it wasn't just his touch that sliced away at her reserve, it was his genuine courtesy. Cameron's thoughtful, simple gestures were as much a part of him as those searing kisses. Yet it wasn't manners that attracted her, but the core of the man they revealed. He thought of others with a generosity of spirit, without taking away time or love from his family. He hadn't even blamed the Senator or Jess Parker for not checking out the security guards more carefully.

Alexa knew many important men. Many were so consumed with business that they didn't have time to worry about their children. And the men who didn't strive to succeed had never interested Alexa. However, Cameron was a complex mix of hard businessman and compassionate father. He clearly adored medicine and yet he had no compunction about putting off starting his practice until he'd assured his sons' safety. She admired that trait in him most of all—his commitment to family.

And she liked the entire family. The oldest brother, Tyler, was quiet, but he'd made her feel welcome. Chase was like the brother she'd always wanted—steady, a good father and totally in love with his wife—while Rafe was the charming youngster who would someday fall hard for some lucky woman. And the Senator, a class act all his own, ran the family with an iron hand and a soft heart.

The twins couldn't have a better family to grow up in. The judge would have to see the boys belonged here with this vibrant family. And Alexa would always be glad she'd taken the time to get to know them.

Cameron pulled up to a barbed-wire gate and stopped the car. While he got out and opened the gate, she slid behind the wheel and drove through, then waited for him to close the gate and return to the car. Unlike the Sutton ranch that had the luxury of extra acreage, the majority for pastures and small ribbons of land set aside for roads, Bodine's ranch was more modest. Every inch of acreage was used for grazing, right up to the front yard of his trailer.

Boasting exaggerated eaves, the trailer ran parallel to the front yard and had a carport with saddles hanging from the ceiling at one end and a prefab fireplace at the other. The front end had a basic open-air stoop and nearby squatted a thousand-gallon cattle-watering tank that could double as a swimming pool.

Next to a row of puny poplars, a big satellite dish sat in the backyard and provided shade for cows. A faded green pickup truck was parked in the drive. Clearly little time went into the trailer's upkeep.

At the Suttons' ranch, Bodine kept a paddock of perfectly groomed horses, saw to dehorning steers and worming calves with meticulous efficiency, but inside his home, dirty laundry overflowed the hamper and dozens of marks marred the coffee table.

"Excuse the mess." Bodine's housekeeping apology, like big-belt buckles, seemed pretty ubiquitous on a small ranch. He gestured for them to take a seat on the sofa beside a dead plant. "Just move that rope and those spurs to the coffee table. I wasn't expecting company."

"I wanted to ask a few more questions about your knife," Cam said, sitting so close to Alexa that her leg and hip and shoulder were plastered against his hard muscles.

Bodine set out a bowl of chips and handed them each a beer. "Ask away, Doc."

Cameron twisted off the cap, took a long swallow and then played with the icy bottle. "Did any of the men who worked for us ever take special notice of your knife?"

"Not that I can remember."

"That blue handle is very distinctive," Alexa said, hoping to prod Bodine's memory. She kept inching away from Cam on the sofa but sliding right back.

The foreman scratched his head. "Now that I think

on it, Cody once offered to let me bet the knife, instead of a ten-dollar ante, in a poker game.''

Alexa frowned. ''Cody isn't old enough to play poker.''

Cameron and Bodine shared a long look and shrugged in unison. Alexa chose to ignore their mockery. Gambling was illegal, and for the ranch hands to let the teenager participate just wasn't right.

''I take it you didn't wager the knife?'' Cameron asked, casually looping an arm over Alexa's shoulders.

''No, sir. Ray Potter borrowed it once to fillet a fish, but he returned it that same evening. I kept good track of it. My daddy gave me that knife. And his daddy before him.''

''You know the doll seemed old, too. Like an antique,'' Alexa commented, trying to ignore Cameron's physical closeness and his warmth seeping into her.

''What are you getting at, ma'am?''

''I'm not sure. It may mean nothing.'' She couldn't think with Cam sitting so near. She needed air, needed space, but he wasn't giving her any.

''All right, let's try another angle,'' Cam suggested. ''Which men at the ranch have a military or mining background and also had access to my house yesterday?''

''I'm not sure I understand what you're getting at, Doc. Almost everyone had access to your house. It's near the stable, and you never lock it. During the wedding, anyone could have sneaked inside.'' Bodine paused. ''As for the military background, I was a Navy SEAL.''

"So you have knowledge of explosive devices?" Alexa asked, trying to figure out whether or not Bodine's freely made admission made him appear less guilty.

"Some." Bodine held her gaze, and she couldn't believe a Navy SEAL would sell out his employer for a few bucks. Cameron was right. Bodine had more sense than to stab a doll with his own knife and expect to get away with it.

"Have you heard any of the hands complaining about work lately?" Cam asked.

"No more than usual."

"Anyone speculating overly much on my personal business?"

"No, Doc."

"Have any of the hands been spending more money than normal?" Alexa asked, unwilling to let Cam do all the thinking. She crossed her legs, letting her calf rub suggestively against his leg. If he wanted to play touching games, she knew how to play, too.

Bodine's eyes narrowed, and for the first time, he seemed unsure of his answer. "What do you mean?"

"Anyone buy a flashy new car? Or gamble too much? Or uncharacteristically buy a round of drinks at the local bar?" Cameron elaborated.

Bodine closed his eyes, then opened them slowly. "Actually, that new cook, Leo Harley, just bought a spiffy new saddle. One of those expensive ones with silver inlay. And Cody's mom traded in her old Chevy for a newer model. And I just bought another hundred acres to connect to my back forty." Bodine tipped up his beer and downed the rest of the bottle.

Then he wiped his mouth delicately with a cocktail napkin. "So what?"

Alexa leaned forward, letting her hair fall onto Cam's shoulder. "We think my grandparents may be paying off someone to make Cameron look foolish when he goes to court to try and keep custody of his boys."

Bodine's eyes widened in surprise. "You think your own grandparents would—"

"They think they would be better parents than Cameron," Alexa explained. "So we're looking for someone who might take a little money on the side. Maybe this person doesn't even realize the stakes. He may not intend to hurt anyone, may have been paid just to scare me away."

"No one is that dumb," Bodine said. "One other thing I should tell you, Doc. I hate to mention it, but under the circumstances…"

"What?"

"That day, when the bridge blew up…"

"Yeah?"

"I saw another horse and rider out there."

Alexa leaned forward again, practically holding her breath. "Who was it?"

"I didn't get a good look."

"Who do you think it was?"

"I can't be sure. That's why I didn't want to say anything, but I thought…"

"Thought what?" Alexa prodded as she gritted her teeth, thinking pulling information from Bodine was worse than from the twins.

Bodine finally spit out the words. "It looked like the Doc's sister-in-law. Laura Sutton."

Alexa gasped. Her beautiful sister-in-law couldn't have had anything to do with blowing up the bridge.

"Maybe Laura was out on an innocent ride," Cam said. His stiff shoulders, tight lips and narrowed eyes said a lot more. Clearly he didn't believe Laura Sutton capable of doing such a thing, either.

"The rider would have heard the explosion," Bodine insisted with a speculative look. "And if so, wouldn't it have been normal to investigate?"

"Maybe Laura didn't hear it. Sound can travel funny over pastureland. Or maybe she was in a hurry," Cam suggested.

"Or maybe it wasn't her," Alexa said, taking his hand and giving it a gentle squeeze of support before asking Bodine another question. "What made you think it was Laura? Are you certain the rider was female? Did she have long blond hair?"

Bodine slumped in his chair. "I'm not sure. The rider was galloping, but doing a slow lope, the kind that eats up the miles, not the hell-bent-for-leather riding that winds a horse fast. The horse was dark, a deep chestnut or a black."

"That's not much to go on. Why did you think it might have been Laura?" Cameron asked, his tone even, but Alexa heard the edge of tension beneath.

"I'm telling you the truth, Doc. I just don't know. It was a fleeting impression, and that's why I hesitated to say anything at all. It could have been a man. I don't specifically remember hair color, but it may have been blond."

Cameron stood and pulled Alexa up with him. They hadn't learned much, but the more they spoke to Bodine, the more convinced she became of the man's honesty.

Cam shook the foreman's hand. "Thanks for the information and for the beer. If you think of anything else…"

"I'll let you know."

"ARE YOU GOING to question Laura?" Alexa asked Cameron once they were back on their horses and riding home, knowing they didn't have much time before they went to court, and they still couldn't prove anything.

"No." Cameron's tone turned hard. "A few years ago, Laura was accused of murdering my brother, Brent. Eventually, it all got sorted out and she was completely exonerated. But those were hard times for her and Chase. I won't cast one iota of suspicion on her."

"She could have been out there having an innocent ride," Alexa said, drawing her horse closer to his.

"Exactly."

"So wouldn't it help to know if she was out there alone or if she saw someone else?"

"We *are* looking for someone else. The subject is closed." His face, hard as flint, had a stubborn cast to the jaw, gray eyes determined to treat his family his way. For an intelligent man, he could be remarkably stubborn and close-minded when it came to his family. Usually she saw this quality as a strength, but it could also be a weakness.

Alexa reached over and touched Cam's shoulder. "Maybe Laura saw something that could help us."

"We aren't going there. Laura is a Sutton."

"And as a Sutton, she'd want to help." Alexa sighed, thinking how easily Cam could ignore her touches. "I'm not saying we have to accuse her of anything."

"We damn well won't." He moved his horse closer to hers as if his dominating presence would make her give in to his argument.

Alexa wouldn't be intimidated. "Did Laura fall apart when she was accused of murder?"

"Of course not."

"She didn't have a nervous breakdown?"

"She's a strong woman."

"And didn't your brother stand by her even when things looked their worst?"

"Of course."

"So neither of them would fall apart if we asked a few simple—"

"I said no." Cam increased the pace to a canter, his horse kicking up clouds of dust.

Alexa dug her heels into her horse, encouraging the animal to stay even with Cameron's mount. "You're being unreasonable."

"And you're being argumentative."

"That's because you're wrong."

"It won't be the first time," he said so mildly she wanted to slap him. How could she argue with him when he'd just agreed with her?

Damn him! He'd been touching her all day, making her edgy as hell. Then he tried to avoid the conversation, and when she wouldn't let him, he'd just ended it by saying he'd made the decision, and that was that. While Alexa admired his absolute faith in

Laura's innocence and his determination to protect his sister-in-law from anything unpleasant, she didn't agree with his thinking.

"Maybe Laura saw something and didn't realize it might be important to us." Frustration made her reckless, and she cut off his horse, forcing him to a stop.

"We'll manage without questioning Laura."

Slightly out of breath from anger more than exertion, Alexa glared at him. "Does anyone ever win an argument with you?"

When he reached over, grabbed her waist and plucked her from the saddle, she was too astonished to do more than sputter. "Just w-what—"

His mouth came down on hers, cutting off her words. Her palms slammed into his hard chest and she jerked her head back. "I'm not kissing you back."

He gathered her closer. "Sure you are, darling."

"I'm not your darl—" His hands came up over her breasts and she responded immediately. Not only did he notice, his thumbs tweaked her aroused nipples maddeningly.

She couldn't stop her physical reaction, and that only increased her anger. How dare he treat her like this? He couldn't win the argument, so he wanted to kiss her into submission?

Not this woman. But why did he have to feel so good? He knew exactly what she liked—seemingly instinctively, his fingers found sensitive spots, his mouth was magic, and her thoughts spun dangerously out of control. Her back arched and she barely bit back a soft moan of delight.

"You want me as much as I want you." His mouth came down on hers again, taking, demanding, and shooting darts of pleasure through her.

She wanted him, all right. But she couldn't decide if she wanted to kiss him or kick him. Out of nowhere, he had her hot as a branding iron ready to burn, and that he could affect her so easily was downright humiliating.

She twined her fingers into his hair, yanked his head back and locked gazes with him. "Are you out of your mind?"

"That's the effect you have on me. You're making me crazy. Crazy for you."

"I've married a lunatic."

He nibbled on her ear. "Lucky for you, they haven't locked me up yet."

"Arrogant man." His tiny nibbles were doing odd things to her erratic pulse. She actually felt light-headed and excited. "I'm not making love on a horse."

Cameron let out a low, husky growl and dismounted. He yanked a bedroll from behind his saddle, unfurled it, wrapped his arms around her and toppled her with him to the blanket.

"Now, where were we?"

"You were about to let me tear off your clothes," she teased, unbuttoning his shirt and exposing his broad chest.

She twirled her fingers through the light dusting of curls, gratified to see his breathing change in response to her slightest caress. Beneath her white fingertips, his tanned flesh was sleek, hard and hot.

He didn't give her much time to explore, drawing

her lips back to his and tugging her shirt out of her slacks, unfastening her bra. "I've been wanting to do this since the day you took that mud bath and showered in the horse stall," he muttered.

"What?"

"Didn't you know what you were doing to me?"

She nuzzled the soft skin at his neck, liked the feel of his breath by her ear. "What?"

"You were naked and I wanted to peek."

"Did you?" she murmured as she unbuckled his belt and shoved his jeans and boxers to his knees.

He kicked his pants the rest of the way off and removed her slacks and panties. "I should have. I've been wondering what you looked like with your clothes off."

"And now you know."

"I haven't seen anything yet." He pulled back and his gaze moved over her hungrily, his eyes kindled and smoked. "Wow!"

His hot look urged her on to a boldness she'd never known. She arched her back and flicked her hair over her shoulder, letting him feast his eyes on her breasts. She actually felt herself warming, swelling, under his gaze. She'd never felt so feminine. Never felt so eager to know a man. She wanted to learn him by feel, memorize the silky texture of hair over solid muscle, taste the salty musk that intoxicated her like a fine wine.

For a big man, he didn't carry a spare inch of fat. Cameron was all lean muscle and broad bones.

She breathed in his scent, a heady combination of sweet grass, leather and spice. Her tongue lapped at the soft spot between his neck and collarbone, and he bucked under her, impatient for her weight.

Then his head rose and he captured the tip of one breast between his teeth. Hot, sizzling sensation seared her. Her head arced backward as she gasped in sheer pleasure.

She straddled him, but he held her captured in limbo with his teeth and tongue, creating exquisite sensations, like soft rain on a gentle breeze. He took her bottom in his big hands, spreading her legs wider until his fingers slipped between her legs.

"Darling, you caught me unprepared. I didn't bring protection."

A fleeting sadness washed over her, only to disappear in a moment. "It's taken care of." She reached behind her and found him thick and hard and waiting.

He groaned, hot and heavy and deliciously ready for her. "Have mercy, woman."

She wanted to make him wait. She wanted to make him as wild as he'd made her. But she couldn't stand the sensations beating at her, urging her onward, making her crazy with need for him. She shifted her weight. He slid inside her smoothly, and she took him with an ease that showed how ready she was for him.

"You feel too good," she whispered, experimentally flexing a muscle.

"Hold still, sweetheart," he ordered, sweat beading on his forehead.

She grinned her most wicked grin. "Not a chance, beefcake." Rocking her hips, she gyrated, taking pleasure in how he was trying to hold back, liking the power she had over him.

Control ended all too soon. Cam's hands slid to her bottom again, and he reversed their positions in the blink of an eye. Suddenly he was on top, driving into her. She wrapped her legs around him, welcoming each thrust, urging him deeper.

His hips lunged downward and she matched him move for move, wrapping her arms around his chest, her nails clawing at his back. And when he took her over the edge, he went with her, his shout letting her know his pleasure.

But Cameron wasn't done. Although his heart pounded against her chest, although his flesh was slick with sweat, he gathered her close, holding her as if she were a fragile piece of glass. He fondled and caressed and massaged. At his tenderness, sweet emotions threatened to lift her into a state where she believed anything was possible.

She considered staying here, wrapped in Cam's arms and letting their marriage become real. As he held her gently, she knew they'd just shared something precious, something that shouldn't be wasted. Her bones felt like melted butter, and her thoughts drifted around the fact that staying with Cam might be her one chance to have a family.

She had to admit she felt remarkably content. And she sensed her cousin Sandra would have approved. But was that enough to start a life together? She'd always enjoyed her independent lifestyle, traveling, work. But she'd never before felt she had other options. After her terrible experience with Wyatt, she'd never again placed herself in a situation where she had to consider any other kind of life.

Alexa was surprised to find contentment here playing the pretend wife, sharing Cam's children. But she had no idea if these feelings for Cam could last, and even thinking about how she felt scared her. She hadn't wanted to become too attached to him and the twins, but she'd ended up making love to him, ended up adoring his children. And when the time came, leaving would just about break her heart.

Even if she wanted to stay for a while, she shouldn't let the twins become too close to her or her to them. She'd miss Cam, too. Making love to him had been indescribably delicious, and she didn't regret their actions, no matter how hard it would be to leave.

Cam smoothed back a stray lock of hair from her face. "I'd like you to stay with us, Alexa."

Chapter Ten

"What do you mean?" Alexa asked, a soft hitch in her voice.

"We're good together," Cam said, stating the obvious. Ever since Alexa had arrived in his life, the sky had seemed bluer, steak had tasted better, music had sounded sweeter. He felt more alive, more alert than he had since he'd been married to Sandra. And though he'd always love his first wife, he loved Alexa differently.

"I hardly think one good romp in a cow pasture qualifies as a basis for me to stay, Cam."

Beneath her tone, he heard a purr of satisfaction, but also a hint of unease. Just because she fit so well into his family didn't mean she wanted to stay, he reminded himself. Although he might not have the twins if he lost them in tomorrow's court case, he'd fight one battle at a time. Cam wouldn't let her go without a fight—not after what they had just shared.

Already he wanted to taste her again, run his fingers through her silky hair, feel her nestled against his chest. She fit him physically, her long lean legs wrapping around him, her head tucked under his chin, her fingernails lightly raking his back. She matched him emotionally, their passions equally fervent. Lord, kissing her was like having peach cobbler drizzled with brown sugar and whipped cream.

He'd merely tapped the surface of the passion he'd sensed in her. A swirling maelstrom lay below the poised veneer she presented to the world, and he couldn't wait to delve into those feelings again. But already, she was erecting walls.

He twirled a piece of her hair around his finger. "You like the boys."

"What's not to like?" Her voice remained light, but she tensed, her muscles taut across her shoulders and neck.

"And you must like me just a little."

"I like lots of men."

He bristled that she would place him in the same category as other men, implying there had been so many in her life. He knew better. Sandra had often worried that her cousin would never find the right man, because she wouldn't let any man into her life. Nor did he believe Alexa could treat what they'd just experienced as a casual encounter. Couldn't she feel the attraction between them? Surely it wasn't just one-sided.

He tried to think rationally. She'd told him he needn't use protection. Did that mean Sandra had been wrong, that Alexa kept herself prepared for a serendipitous affair whenever she had an itch? He didn't believe it. Alexa wasn't the kind of woman to be satisfied with a one-night-stand or a short-term lover.

And he was guessing she'd used that last statement

to put him off. But it wouldn't work. He didn't care
about the men in her past. He only cared that there
would be one man in her future—him.

"But you like me the best," he concluded as his
hand closed over her breast, which reacted immediately to his caress.

"Women don't rate men on scales of one to ten,"
Alexa told him, without pulling away. "But if you
want me to tell you how good it was, I will."

"I'm not looking for a compliment but a commitment."

Alexa sat up and fumbled for her clothes, her face
flushed. She avoided looking at him. "That wasn't
the deal."

A moment ago, she'd been as relaxed as a cat
snoozing in the sun. Now she needed clothes to put
another barrier between them.

He let her dress but didn't bother doing so himself.
Instead, he rolled to his back and laced his fingers
behind his head. "What's wrong with changing our
agreement? Making our marriage a real one?"

"You don't want me."

Of all the responses Alexa could have given him,
that had to be the lamest. He damn well knew what
he wanted. And he wanted her.

He rolled to his side and raised himself on his bent
elbow. "Why don't you think I want you?"

"Do you want more children? A sweet little
brother or sister for Jason and Flynn?"

Cam watched her pale, saw her fingers clench,
noted the tight cord of distress in her tone. Anguish
flickered in her beautiful eyes, and he realized she
was torn up inside. And suddenly it hit him.

Alexa couldn't have children.

That was why she didn't worry about protection. And from the tense way she was holding herself, he sensed his next words were crucial to their future.

"I haven't thought that far ahead," he said slowly.

Cam wouldn't lie to Alexa, nor would he lie to himself. A big family had never been his dream, but he'd always just sort of assumed he would have more children someday.

As if she could read his thoughts, Alexa straightened her spine and fisted her hands on her hips. "I can't have children, Cam. My ovaries are gone, so don't start thinking about medical miracles. It won't happen."

She'd finished dressing and stood looking down at him. Cold, self-possessed, calm. And he wondered how much it cost her to act as if she didn't care. Cam held out his hand to her. She hesitated for a moment and then let him draw her against his side.

She sat with her back to his chest, leaning against him, and, dry-eyed, stared off at the horizon. "Don't feel pity for me. I lost the ovaries when I was sixteen, long before the age when most women decide they want kids. I simply changed my life into a direction that satisfied me. I'm happy, Cam."

She didn't sound happy. She sounded drained and emotionally spent. And all he could think about was wiping that wan look off her face.

"Jason and Flynn are such a handful it might not be fair to them to have other children. But adoption is always a possibility. I really don't see what having children or not has to do with your agreeing to stay."

"Because if you want more children, and you

probably will, I won't be able to give them to you. It's hard to find babies to adopt. And could you feel the same way about them as your own—"

His voice hardened. "Don't go there. Dad adopted Brent, and I loved him just as much as my other brothers. After his murder, I sure as hell didn't console myself by saying he wasn't my biological brother. I loved him just as much as Tyler and Chase and Rafe. The good thing about love is that it's limitless. For the right people, there's always enough to go around."

"Even if you feel this way now, you may change your mind and grow to resent me. You can't know the future. It's just not that simple. "

"It is. I want you, Alexa. If we can't have more children, I can live with that."

Cam hoped she could hear the truth in his words. He wouldn't have said them if they weren't true. He had too much respect for Alexa to lie to her about an issue this important. A family of four would satisfy him just fine.

Her fingers twisted the plain gold wedding band around her finger as if it was a shackle. "I don't want you to have to settle for less."

"Alexa, I already have two healthy boys. What I need to complete my family is a woman I love. And that woman is you."

He'd just laid his heart open to her, and she didn't say a word. The silence sliced and diced his emotions raw, but he waited through the pain, knowing that however this discussion ended, he wouldn't give up. He'd woo her, wine her and dine her and make love to her until she agreed to spend the rest of her life with him. Cameron Sutton considered his best quality to be sheer stubbornness. And no matter what Alexa said, no matter how much she denied it, she was going to like being married to him. He'd make sure of it.

She swiveled to face him, her eyes brimming with unshed tears. "I don't know what to say."

He read the confusion in her gaze and kissed her gently on the lips. "You don't have to decide now. Think about it. Think about having a family and living here with me and Jason and Flynn. We need you, Alexa. We want you."

"I need time to think."

"So I'll give you a moment or two," he teased lightly. He didn't want her to think. He wanted her to feel. To let herself go where she hadn't gone before.

One tear escaped down her cheek. "You're very good with words."

With his thumb, he smoothed away the tear, kissed her forehead, her nose, her mouth. He reached for her shirt, ducked his head under it and murmured, "That's not all I'm good with."

ALEXA REPAIRED her hair, tucked her shirt back in and reapplied lipstick, blush and mascara. However, she couldn't make her feelings return to the way they were before she and Cameron had made love. During the ride back, Cameron didn't try to sway her. In fact, he seemed content to let her think about what had happened between them and the future he'd dangled in front of her like a big juicy plum.

Alexa didn't know what to think or how to decide.

Indecision swamped her. How could she believe
Cameron knew what he wanted? Clearly he thought
he was telling her the truth about being content with
just the twins, but suppose he changed his mind? He
would come to resent her. Yet because he was such
an honorable man, he'd never say anything, just let
regrets eat away at him until their relationship cor-
roded.

And even if Cameron meant what he'd said, Alexa
didn't know if she wanted what he was offering. She
already loved the twins. But did she want to be their
mother? It was a huge commitment and one she
needed to consider carefully.

How much would she miss her work, and what
would she replace it with? Alexa had no idea. Work
had kept her too busy to develop hobbies to fall back
on, and being a mother full-time wasn't enough to
keep her satisfied. She thrived on the chase of a rare
piece of art, the satisfaction of acquiring great art for
her clients.

And she didn't know if she was falling in love
with Cameron. She might be. She liked him. She
respected him. And she'd never met a man who
could turn her on with just a look. But was that love?

Confused, Alexa's thoughts swirled as she tried to
use logic to evaluate every angle. She told herself
this might be her only chance to have a family—but
was that what she wanted?

Alexa had a good life, a career many envied and
friends in every major city in the world. To give that
up to become a doctor's wife and live on a ranch in
Colorado was a drastic change. She needed to consider it carefully.

Cameron had said he would give her time, so the only pressure she had was what she put on herself. But indecision didn't sit well with Alexa. She liked to know what she wanted and then work to achieve it. This uncertainty was akin to swimming in the ocean without a place to put your feet down and rest.

Cameron rode toward the stable, and Alexa's horse needed little direction from her to follow. They unsaddled the horses and turned them over to a groom. Cam carried the tack to the equipment room, and Alexa walked behind him, breathing in the fresh scent of hay, manure and oats.

The tack room, neat as the Barringtons' Boston living room, boasted an assortment of saddles, bridles and hackamores. Stirrups, bits of leather and horseshoes hung on pegs on one wall.

Since arriving on the ranch, Alexa had learned some interesting cowboy customs from Cameron. A hand's saddle was always the best he could afford. A little stamping or carving on the leather added character. And with two-inch boot heels and jingling spurs, the cowboy's yen for flash could often be seen when they went into town.

She could probably borrow a cowboy's gun if she needed to, and for a good enough reason she could borrow his horse. But it was unthinkable to ask to borrow his saddle, since it was a part of him that was near sacred.

The Senator kept the horse that Cameron had lent her for guests. Same with the saddle. As Cameron hung the gear on pegs and slung the saddles over wooden benches, Alexa heard an odd zap. Like static electricity, only louder.

"Did you hear—"

Cam grabbed her and thrust her through the tack room's back door. "Run!"

The urgency in his tone, the force of his hands propelling her body, hastened her footsteps. Her pulse skyrocketed at the danger he sensed, but she didn't see anything wrong.

He didn't wait to see whether she listened to him. Taking her hand, he yanked her out of the barn and half-pulled, half-carried her into the yard.

A sudden roar, then a blast of hot wind, sent Alexa tumbling to her knees, her stomach. Beneath her, the ground bucked.

Then Cam flattened her, his big body covering her, protecting her from flying debris. Smoke filled her nostrils and horses screamed in fear. Alexa turned her head toward the stable and saw flames leaping skyward.

"You okay?" Cam asked, rolling off her with the agility of a mountain cat.

She stood, horrified at the flames licking their way from the tack room toward the stalls. "The horses!"

His measured look seemed to assure him that she wasn't injured, and Cam started to run toward the stable, yelling back over his shoulder, "Get help."

Alexa turned to do as he asked, but the noise from the explosion had already warned everyone of the danger. Men came running from all directions— sheds, paddocks, Cameron's house and the open range. But she and Cam were closest.

Without hesitating, she raced after Cam. Dodging fiery debris and hellish flames shooting out a window, she sprinted around to the far side of the stable.

The groom jammed open the double doors and shooed two horses out by flapping a blanket. An overhead sprinkler system came on, but instead of dousing the flames, the fire worsened and the smoke thickened. Alexa thought she saw Leo hooking up a hose, but couldn't be sure. Surely Leo couldn't have made it from the house to the barn yet, but she could have sworn she saw him through the smoke for an instant.

Holding her arm over her mouth and breathing through her shirt, Alexa ran from stall to stall, opening the doors and hoping the animals would have the sense to flee. As Alexa slipped into the stall where the twins kept their ponies, Cameron smacked a horse on the rump and sent it fleeing to safety.

"Get out of here. The roof's going to collapse," Cameron ordered.

She couldn't abandon the twins' ponies. Alexa hurried to their stall and shoved back the door. She eased toward the frightened horses, then backed them slowly out of the stall. The animals snorted at the smoke and their eyes rolled with terror.

"Come on, boys," she crooned. "That's the way. A few more steps." She kept talking reassuringly until the ponies cleared the stall, then slapped them on the rumps to shoo them outside.

Freeing all the animals was taking too long. Many of the other horses snorted in fear in their stalls, too terrified to leave. The groom headed past Alexa and shifted between a roan and a gray. "Move aside."

Alexa stepped into a nearby stall. The groom slapped the animals on the rump, and they took off for the open doors at a gallop.

Alexa knew the hands would round up the horses later, and she'd just turned to leave when she realized that she'd ducked into the stall where Rafe kept his prize stallion. When the chestnut with white hooves and face spotted her, the frightened animal reared up, whites of his eyes rolling, hooves flailing.

"It's okay, fella. Calm down. I'll get you out of here. Just let me put a hand on your mane and I'll lead you to green grasses, cool water and mares. You'd like that, wouldn't you, boy?"

She spoke softly, knowing the words didn't matter and that the terrified horse probably wouldn't calm down from the sound of her voice, either. But she had to try. She couldn't leave him to burn. But the temperamental animal didn't want anything to do with a stranger.

Alexa ignored the crackle overhead, concentrated on the horse. She needed to throw something over the horse's head so he couldn't see the flames. The thick smoke blinded her and she gave up on finding a blanket. Quickly, she unfastened her blouse, dipped it in the water trough. As the leery animal scooted to one side, she moved in and threw the blouse over his head.

He reared, spun. Knocked her against the wall.

She sprang back and grabbed a handful of her shirt and his mane. "Whoa, boy."

The horse trembled but he didn't buck again. Alexa spared him a moment and rubbed his nose, then tugged on his mane. Inch by inch, she coaxed him out of the stall.

She could hear other voices, hooves clopping down the passageway. Help had arrived. Other hands led out horses, but she couldn't see much in the smoke. She tried to call for help, but her throat was so raw, her voice came out like a croak.

The stallion banged her against a rail, and she almost lost her grip. Overhead, a huge sheet of flames flared, eating through the roof. Beams behind her collapsed.

They had to get out. Now.

And she needed the horse's speed as much as he needed her guidance.

Knowing the animal might buck her off, knowing she couldn't hold on without bridle and saddle, Alexa made a desperate choice. In one awkward move, she flung herself onto the stallion's back, used his mane to pull herself upright and slapped his hind quarters. The powerful stallion needed no further urging.

Muscular hindquarters gathered and thrust forward. And Alexa guided him with her knees, praying she remembered the way out. The stallion lunged forward, and suddenly they burst past the double doors. She glimpsed Leo, Cody, Rafe and Cameron.

Cameron shouted her name as she and the stallion bolted out. Behind them the roof caved in with a crash.

With no bridle and no saddle, Alexa had no way to control the stallion, and he accelerated from zero to thirty in mere seconds. As his hooves pounded the pasture, she hung on to his mane for dear life, gripping his smooth flanks as best she could with her knees.

Wind whipped the hair from her face and she could barely see. The horse tossed his head and her blouse soared behind them. She had no reins to stop the stallion's wild run across the pasture and considered throwing herself to the ground.

Beneath his flying hooves, she saw rocks and reconsidered. How long would it take the animal to tire?

Yanking on his mane did little to stop his terrified dash. She tried talking softly to him but doubted he could hear her through the sound of his hammering hooves.

She heard shouts behind her but didn't dare turn to look. The animal's back became slick with his sweat and she squeezed her knees tighter, hoping she could hang on long enough, but the horse had been bred to run. He didn't even sound winded.

She tried not to think what would happen if he stepped in a hole, tried not to think of pitching over his head and him trampling her.

"Hang on." Cameron's voice, surprisingly close behind her gave her added strength. "We're coming."

Out of the corner of her eyes, she saw two horses and riders closing on her, sandwiching her runaway horse between them. Cam neared on her right, and one of his brothers, Rafe, maybe, on her left.

"Hurry, Cam! I'm slipping!"

"ALMOST THERE." Cam rode next to her, knee to knee, and then he looped one arm around her just as Rafe threw a lasso over the stallion's neck.

Soon. Soon she would be safe.

Until the moment he'd spied Alexa on the stallion's back racing out of the burning barn, he'd had no idea she'd disobeyed him. Instead of going for help, she'd entered the burning building, and in all the confusion and smoke he'd never seen her. Until she rode out like some wild Valkyrie and almost shocked him into a panic.

He and Rafe had lost precious moments, grabbing mounts and going after her. Finally they'd caught up. The two brothers worked together, and slowly the stallion's pace wound down to a canter, then a trot and finally a walk.

In the moonlight, Alexa's face looked as pale as the rising moon. But she tossed her hair over her shoulder, straightened her back, and asked, her tone almost jaunty, "What took you guys so long?"

Rafe chuckled. "Lady, that was some ride. Did you know this horse has never had a rider on his back? I keep him for breeding."

At Rafe's words, Cam's stomach churned. She could have been stomped to death, bucked off and broken her neck. His hands started to tremble, and he felt a little sick at the thought of what could have happened.

Alexa finally seemed to realize the risk she'd taken. "I'd like to get down now."

Cam lifted her from the stallion and placed her on the horse in front of him. She was either trembling from the aftershock or shivering from the cold. He removed his shirt and wrapped her in it. Then his arms closed around her, and he kissed her behind the ear. "Better?"

"Mm."

"Whatever possessed you to climb on his back?" Rafe asked as he led the stallion behind his mount.

"At the time, it seemed the fastest way out of the barn."

"Well, I appreciate your efforts. We left him for last because he's...difficult."

"Difficult!" Cameron exclaimed. "How many times has Bodine told you to shoot the beast? He's a killer."

Alexa leaned against Cam for strength. "He saved my life. And he's as fast as the wind. I'm surprised you caught me."

"We almost didn't," Cam muttered, the fear for her still burning through his stomach. "You shouldn't have risked your life—not even for a million-dollar piece of horseflesh."

Alexa looked behind her at the prancing stallion. "I didn't know the flames would spread so quickly. The sprinklers came on, but they didn't seem to help much."

Rafe cursed under his breath. "Someone turned off the water valve."

Another act of sabotage.

"What caused the explosion?" Alexa asked, her voice still a little shaky.

"We don't know." Cam's arm tightened around her waist. "But I'm betting the explosive device was similar to the one used on the bridge. Someone doesn't want us to make it to the custody trial tomorrow. I hate to accuse them, but the Barringtons have the most to gain from our deaths."

Cam felt Alexa stiffen and could almost feel her working up an automatic protest, but somewhere inside her, it died. Although she didn't believe her grandparents would try to kill her, he couldn't come up with a single other alternative that fit the facts. There'd been trouble since the first day she'd arrived. First the bull had escaped and almost gored her. Then those security guards had drugged her and tried to take the twins. And the bridge and barn had been blown up. Each incident could be used against them at the custody hearing in court, tomorrow.

Cam knew Alexa had never believed her grandparents would fight this dirty, endanger her life, but now she *had* to believe it since no other explanation made sense. He couldn't imagine the sorrow she must feel at the knowledge her only living relatives had turned against her. But she had a new family now. One that would appreciate her, cherish her, protect her.

As they rode back to the Sutton's stable, now a mass of smoking beams and ashes, the air reeked. The building was a total loss, but at least all the animals had been saved.

The Senator, Chase, Tyler and Laura met them on horseback as they rode up. The Senator's face was tight and his eyes glinted with anger and sadness. "Damn stable has too many bad memories."

Brent, Cam's oldest brother, had died in that stable. Tyler had had a terrible accident there, too. Perhaps it would be best to rebuild on another spot.

"I've already called the sheriff," Chase told them. "At least the bridge is back up."

A car pulled down the road and the headlights caught them in the glare before the driver shut them off. Alexa's grandparents exited the vehicle, stared at the smoking stable and then back at Alexa.

Her grandmother, Emily Barrington, frowned at her. "My dear, that shirt is too large for you."

"She's lucky to be alive," Cam practically growled. He wanted to throttle the old woman for giving Alexa any grief after what she'd just been through.

The old man, Dalton, frowned. "You aren't taking very good care of my granddaughter, young man."

"I don't need anyone to take care of me," Alexa protested. "But I'd like to know how long ago you two left the Senator's house."

"There's nothing to do at night," Emily complained. "No shows, no opera, no parties. So we went for a little drive, but there's nothing to see except cows."

At the old woman's admission that they'd been out driving, Alexa's face hardened, but her eyes burned with grief. Clearly she was thinking her grandparents could have set off the explosive device.

"Would you mind if I search your vehicle, sir?" Tyler asked politely, but flint sharpened his tone.

"Are you accusing *me* of something?" Dalton's tone rose in outrage.

The Senator stepped forward. "We think a trigger device set off the explosion and caused the fire. We'd like to make sure you don't have one on you."

Emily Barrington's jaw dropped open and she staggered a step backward. Dalton pounded his cane into the dirt and then at Cameron. "If you accuse me again, I'll take you to court for slander." The old man's face darkened with rage. "Don't blame us if you can't protect your family." He took Emily's arm. "And let me assure you that the judge will hear about this unfounded accusation. With all the goings-on around here, you aren't fit to raise my great-grandchildren. The judge will see things my way, so I'd suggest you start packing their belongings.''

"Don't listen to him," Alexa whispered. "He's all bluster."

Cameron took comfort in her words and in her soft body against him. He could only pray that the old man was wrong.

Chapter Eleven

Cam didn't sleep well the night before the custody hearing and knew dark circles underlined his eyes that morning, but as usual, Alexa, in a blue silk suit, looked luminous enough for them both. She seemed to light the courtroom. Her fair skin, lightly tanned, glowed with well-being, which protected her from the scowls and frowns of her grandparents.

The Barringtons' attorney presented his case first, and even Cam had to admit the evidence against him sounded damning. Their attorney, a sophisticated smooth talker with a dignified air, twisted the facts, bringing up numerous incidents that had occurred since Sandra's death and painting Cameron darker than a moonless night. Apparently the Barringtons' strategy was to smear his name until the judge ruled him unfit.

When the judge heard how the twins had repeatedly been in danger, Cam's heart sank. He'd known these issues would come up, but he hadn't realized how bad they would sound.

Beside him Alexa squeezed his hand, her chin cocked with confidence. ''Just wait for our turn.''

Cam feared that the damage done to his reputation couldn't be reversed. Although Alexa had spent an inordinate amount of time talking with Cam's attorney in private, his hopes started to plummet.

His entire family sat on his side of the courtroom, and Cameron appreciated the solid show of support. But the thought of losing the twins left his palms sweaty and his pulse unsteady.

Finally Alexa took the stand. She didn't rush and kept her gaze on Cam as the bailiff swore her in.

Cam's attorney, Drake Francis, one of Denver's top lawyers had flown in this morning. He offered Alexa a glass of water, then asked her what her relationship to the twins was.

Alexa's voice was cool, direct and businesslike. ''I'm their mother's cousin and their mother by marriage.''

''What prompted you to marry the week before the custody hearing, Mrs. Sutton?'' Francis asked.

''I promised my cousin I wouldn't let our grandparents raise the twins.''

''So you married the father?''

''We thought a couple would have a better chance of keeping the twins than a single father.''

''Tell me about the promise you made to the former Mrs. Sutton.''

''She was dying and she knew it.'' Alexa cleared her throat and pain flared in her eyes. ''She begged me to make sure our grandparents would never raise her boys.''

''And why is that?''

''The Barringtons were our grandparents and they raised Sandra and me.''

"Were you abused?"

Alexa shook her head, a lock of her dark hair falling forward onto her cheek, and Cameron couldn't help but recall the soft silky texture of it. "Sandra didn't want her children to be raised with nannies and then sent to boarding school like we were. She wanted them raised with love."

"Do you love the boys?"

"Yes."

"If you have other children, will you be able to love Flynn and Jason as much as your own?"

"That won't ever be a problem because I can't have children."

"Please, tell us about the man you married. What kind of father is he?"

"He's the kind of father every child could wish for. He's smart and generous with his time. He keeps the boys in line with a kind heart and a loving soul. Sandra wanted Cameron to raise their children, and no one has the right to take that away from him." Alexa stared down her grandparents. "No one."

"Now these incidents that opposing counsel brought up, could you tell us what's happening out at the ranch?"

"We don't know." Alexa's honesty and integrity rang in her tone, and the judge paid attention to her every word. She kept her chin up, her shoulders squared. "Because the trouble began around the same time as the custody battle, we could only assume that someone needed to make Cameron look bad so my grandparents could use the evidence against him in this court."

"Your grandparents are getting on in years, Mrs.

Sutton. Why do you think they are fighting for custody?"

"The boys have a very large trust fund. The Barringtons don't wish to give up the administration of such a vast amount of money."

Emily Barrington gasped aloud as if the mention of money was akin to muttering a curse.

"And why is giving up administration of the trust such a big deal?"

"For one, because they are courted and entertained due to the contributions to charity they make in the boys' names. And second, they don't like to give up anything. They consider it a defeat."

"Are you worried about the boys' safety?" the attorney asked.

"Yes. But once this issue is settled, I expect the danger to be over."

"Thank you, Mrs. Sutton. No more questions, Your Honor."

Opposing counsel for the plaintiffs stood and stepped forward. "Well, I have several."

"Go ahead, sir," the judge said.

Alexa's demeanor didn't change. Although opposing counsel appeared ready to tear her to shreds, she kept her composure.

"How do you feel about your grandparents, Mrs. Sutton?"

"What do you mean?" Alexa asked, her beautiful blue eyes wary, her hands clasped together, each glossy nail a perfect foil for the agitation Cam sensed beneath her calm poise.

"They raised you, and you turned out okay, didn't you?"

"Yes. And if you want to know if I think my grandparents did the best they could, again my answer is yes. But Cameron and I can raise the twins better."

"Do you love your husband, Mrs. Sutton?"

Cameron saw her eyes flicker, and she hesitated for just a second. Clearly she didn't want to answer the question under oath.

But she spoke smoothly and he'd doubted anyone but him could guess how much she didn't want to answer the question. "I love seeing Cameron play with the boys. I love listening to him talk about his passion for medicine. And the love between him and his brothers colors everything the family does. The twins won't be getting just a father and mother, they'll be getting loving aunts and uncles, cousins and—"

"Do you love your husband, Mrs. Sutton?" The attorney pressed her, sensing a weakness he could capitalize on.

Cam's attorney stood. "Objection, Your Honor. I fail to see the relevance—"

"Overruled. Answer the question Mrs. Sutton," the judge said.

When Alexa didn't answer immediately, the courtroom fidgeting stopped. No one whispered or coughed, rattled a paper or so much as shifted in their seat. It was quiet enough to hear a pin drop.

"Let me remind you that you're under oath, Mrs. Sutton," the Barringtons' attorney said.

"I'm aware of that," Alexa snapped. She looked at her grandparents and then back at Cameron and his gut clenched. "Yes. I love my husband."

After that, the case moved easily through each of his brothers' testimony, and by the time the Senator took the stand, it was practically a done deal. However good Alexa had been on the witness stand, her words gnawed at Cameron. Was Alexa telling the truth when she'd said she loved him? The doubt disturbed him. He'd thought they were on their way to a good and passionate marriage, but suppose Alexa had lied so he could keep the twins?

He'd found her courage admirable. And yet he'd wished she could have responded without hesitation. Cam liked being a husband. He liked being part of a family and he liked being married.

Those poor determined-to-remain-bachelors, afraid-to-commit men didn't know what they were missing. Family was everything, and without it, a man had no place to root himself in the world. Even though Cam was a doctor, he simply couldn't imagine delivering a baby or saving a life and never having someone to come home to and share the joy with. He liked intimacy, liked sharing, liked loving.

And he'd married a woman who didn't know what she wanted.

THE SENATOR HAD INVITED the family over for a celebration dinner after the judge ruled the twins would stay with their father and new mother.

The parting scene with her grandparents had been painful for Alexa. No hugs. No goodbyes. Just hurtful glances because she had implied they were behind the series of problems on the ranch.

And now Alexa stood in front of her newly finished closet, her nose screwed up at the scent of fresh

paint and wallpaper paste, deciding what to wear.
Her silk black skirt and black wraparound top
seemed too casual for the occasion, her white beaded
pantsuit, too formal.

Cam stuck his head through the door to her room.
"Hurry up, sweetheart. The twins will need another
bath if you don't decide soon."

Alexa groaned. "I should have called Laura and
asked her what she was wearing."

"Something sexy. She wants another child, and
she's determined to make Chase so crazy he'll forget
how hard the last childbirth was on her."

"You're a big help."

Cameron stepped into the room, wearing a black
sports jacket that emphasized his broad shoulders
over a black sweater with black jeans that made his
long legs seem even longer. His gray eyes perused
hers, and then his sooty lashes swept down to hide
his thoughts. "I'm sorry. I shouldn't have thrown
Laura's wanting a third baby in your face."

Taking her cue from Cam's elegantly casual attire,
Alexa finally pulled out a red blouse and the black
skirt and donned them over her slip. "I'm not that
sensitive. I suspect the twins are just about all I can
handle. So you don't need to tiptoe around the subject of children, okay? If Laura has another baby, I'll
be happy for her."

Cam's nostrils flared just before his eyes turned to
smoke. And she knew he was going to kiss her. Anticipation heated her. Cam's kisses were worth waiting for, and he'd been remarkably generous with
them since the custody hearing last week. If he'd

been another man, she'd have been sure his mind was bent on seduction.

But Cam had more complicated thoughts. He seemed to have some kind of campaign mapped out to woo her. And she found his intentions not only sexy but invading her dreams at night. Lately her dreams had been erotic, and she kept wondering if he was waiting for her to seduce him.

So she was more than ready for his kiss. A slow heated kiss that had her throwing her arms around his neck and pulling him against her. His spicy aftershave mixed with the scent of his jacket and his natural masculine musk, invading her senses until she wanted to drag him onto her bed and rip off his clothes.

The patter of hushed voices finally wiggled through her consciousness.

"Told you they were kissing." Flynn's loud whisper traveled right through the open door.

Jason sounded as if he'd made a new discovery. "He put his tongue in her mouth."

"That's yucky."

"I saw Uncle Rafe breeding a stallion. The stallion's yang pointed at the moon and he put it right—"

Cam broke their kiss, a smile on his lips. "Boys, we don't discuss the details of breeding horses in front of a lady."

Flynn's little face screwed up with confusion. "But, Dad, Aunt Laura talks about breeding."

Alexa could see that Cameron was at a loss. His inquisitive sons asked the darnedest questions. Restraining a laugh, she decided to help him out.

She smoothed Jason's hair and straightened Flynn's collar. "It's okay to talk about breeding—but only if the lady brings up the subject first."

"Okay, got it." Flynn grinned up at her mischievously. "Are you ready yet? Dad says ladies take a real long time to put on their faces, but yours looks all done and I'm hungry."

Alexa chuckled. "My face doesn't come apart into pieces like one of your puzzles."

"It doesn't?"

"Your father meant it takes me a long time to fix my hair and makeup."

"Your hair is clean." Jason tugged her hand. "Can we go now?"

Cam drove them over to the Senator's, claiming if they went by horseback they'd be late. But Alexa knew the real reason. The kiss had inflamed her senses and aroused Cameron so much that sitting on a horse right now would be uncomfortable.

Alexa liked the passion that sizzled like lightning between them. But what did she really want? Her life had taken a different path the day she'd learned she couldn't have children. She'd made the most of her skills and abilities, but now that a new direction offered itself, the chance to have children and a family, did she want to take it?

Would she have wanted children if she could have had them? Maybe. Alexa didn't know. She most certainly enjoyed the twins. Every time she considered leaving them she thought about how much she'd miss their carefree smiles and delicious hugs, their antics, their curiosity. She loved them.

But did she want to live in Colorado, give up the

reputation she'd built for herself in the art world? Then again, she'd always dreamed of retiring and opening her own art gallery in a tourist town, and Highview certainly had enough tourists to support such an endeavor.

During the drive to the Senator's house, her thoughts drifted as the boys argued over a puzzle in the back seat. It seemed just minutes before they pulled into the Senator's drive.

"Look!" Flynn's excited voice drew Alexa's attention to Rafe, who was leading a frisky colt onto the driveway.

Sunlight gleamed on the colt's black back, but it was the delicately arched neck, the proud lift of the head and the intelligent eyes that drew the entire family out of the car to admire the animal.

Rafe, whipcord lean, and elegant from his gleaming black boots to his freshly combed dark hair, held out the hackamore lead to Alexa. His eyes lit with a rakish twinkle and his mouth quirked. "He's yours."

Alexa gasped.

"He's awesome," Jason said.

Flynn patted his nose. "And friendly."

Alexa stared at the colt's finely shaped head, the ears pricked forward. The animal's graceful neck arched down to well-defined withers, which were in direct line with the croup, the highest point of the rounded and muscled hindquarters. But it was the legs that told her the colt's value, the feet matching one another in size and shape, the legs muscular and lean and long.

Rafe tipped his hat and placed the lead in her hand. "My gift to you for saving his sire."

Surprise took her aback. "I can't accept such a valuable—"

"Take him," Cameron urged her with a slight smile. "My brother will be insulted if you don't."

"But, but…I don't know anything about training such an animal."

"You can learn," Cam said.

"I wouldn't want to make any mistakes with him. He's gorgeous but…"

Alexa tried to give the lead back to Rafe. Rafe only refused it and shook his head. "The cost of boarding shouldn't be much. 'Course there's feeding, shoeing, veterinarian fees, insurance, tack and the costs of traveling to the shows—"

"Shows?"

"—and entry fees if you wish to compete."

"Compete?"

Feeling overwhelmed and knowing she didn't have the knowledge to do this horse justice, she scratched the animal behind the ears, enchanted with the idea of owning a living thing of such beauty. "I'll accept him on one condition."

Rafe and Cameron raised identical eyebrows.

"Is she dumb?" Jason asked. "She can't give him back."

"She's not dumb," Flynn argued. "She's scared."

"Boys—" Cameron's voice turned stern "—what did I tell you about calling anyone dumb?"

"It's rude. Sorry, Lexi." The twins said in unison.

Cameron shrugged. "They have that down a little too pat."

Were her emotions so obvious that two-year-olds, granted extra bright two-year-olds, could see the fear on her face? Alexa refused to accept so valuable an animal when she had no conception of the responsibilities required to care for him.

"What's your condition, Alexa?" Rafe finally asked.

"We go partners on him, fifty-fifty." Alexa held out her hand for Rafe to shake.

Rafe hesitated, looked at Cameron, who nodded slightly, then took her hand. "Partners."

They shook on the deal, and then Rafe motioned for a ranch hand to take the foal back to his mother. Alexa watched the proud prance of the animal and knew, regardless of whether she stayed as Cam's wife, she would come back often to check on the colt's progress.

"She's looking at the colt like she looks at you," Rafe teased Cameron.

"You're just jealous," Cam teased right back.

"Of a horse?"

"Very funny. Now that the partnership's settled, let's go eat." Cameron steered Alexa toward the front door.

Behind them, Rafe took each of the twins by the hand, shortening his long steps to allow them to keep up. "Do you boys know what a partner is?"

Jason frowned. "She gave you back half the horse?"

Flynn's high-pitched voice asked, "Why, Uncle Rafe?"

"Because sometimes when you give away half, you get more than if you kept everything for yourself," Rafe answered patiently.

"I don't get it."

"Me, neither."

"The horse will be more valuable if I train him, because I'm an expert," Rafe told them.

"I want to be an expert."

Alexa took Cam's hand and they entered the house together. Once, she'd felt a stranger here, but now as Laura and Chase, Tyler and the Senator greeted them, and the kids raced toward the dining room, feelings of contentment stole through Alexa. This was the family she'd always wanted.

"Would you like to freshen up?" Laura asked her. "I'll take you upstairs."

After petting the horse, Alexa did want to wash her hands, and she also appreciated the chance to speak to Laura alone. They climbed a carpeted staircase lined with family portraits. No stuffy pictures for the Senator. His pictures were framed shots of little boys riding and playing and growing up on the ranch.

Alexa vowed to study them another time. "There's something I've been wanting to ask you…"

"About Cameron?" Laura's bright green eyes turned to Alexa with a twinkle.

"As a matter of fact, Cameron would be furious with me if he knew I was discussing this with you."

Laura's face broke into a friendly grin. "Sounds interesting. I adore gossip."

Alexa slipped into the first bedroom they came to. "It's something that's bothered me for a long time, and Cameron forbade me to say anything to you, but…"

Laura seemed to realize that Alexa wasn't going to ask some deep secret about Cameron's past but about the recent problems on the ranch, because her face turned serious. "The men in this family tend to be overly protective of me. Sometimes it's great. More often it's a pain in the ass. Talk."

"The day the bridge exploded, Bodine said he saw someone who looked like you riding in the distance." Alexa hesitated. "I just wondered if you saw anybody or anything unusual that day."

Laura's eyes darkened. "Why didn't Cameron just ask me?"

"He didn't want you to think we were accusing you of anything."

"That's ridiculous. I'm not made of glass." Laura stared unseeingly out the window at the green mountains, and Alexa could almost envision her memories turning back to that day. She twisted her fingers through her gorgeous blond hair as she concentrated. "I didn't hear the blast because Julie and I had taken the twins and Keith out for a ride, and Julie had the radio turned up. Leo brought us a picnic basket for lunch. But I didn't see anything unusual."

"Would you have noticed my grandparents' car?" Alexa asked, hoping to put her doubts behind her.

"Maybe. Maybe not. When the twins and Keith get together, you need eyes in the back of your head." Laura repeated Chase's favorite expression with a sigh. "Sorry I can't be more helpful."

"Helpful about what?" Chase wandered into the room, and both women jumped.

Laura gave him a bright smile. "Just woman talk."

Her sister-in-law wasn't a good liar, but Chase

seemed inclined to let it go. He winked at his wife. "I like woman talk."

"And pillow talk," Laura teased him right back, took his arm and led him downstairs.

Relieved at their departure, but jittery and a little ill at ease from going behind Cameron's back to question Laura, Alexa took in several deep breaths. To calm herself, she washed her hands and freshened her makeup, then joined the others for dinner.

As she looked across the table at Cameron and into his shadowed gaze, she knew he suspected the subject of her conversation with Laura. But it wasn't until they'd gone home and tucked the kids into bed that he stopped her at the upstairs landing overlooking the first floor, cornered her and asked, "So what did you and Laura talk about?"

Ignoring his question, she gestured to the finished living area below. The painters and wallpaperers had done a fine job, and the comfortable leather furniture she'd ordered fit in well with the elegant but snug look she'd been striving for. Cam hadn't mentioned whether or not he liked the finished product, nor had he complained about the bill she'd rung up on his credit card.

"You did a great job and I like the way you've turned this place into a home. Now tell me about your conversation with Laura."

Although he was making her feel as if she'd betrayed him, she didn't bother lying. But the conversation was going to cost him. She had a few very expensive pieces of art she wanted to hang on his walls. "Laura told me she and Keith met up with

Julie, Leo and the twins for lunch the day the bridge exploded.''

Cameron stiffened and anger radiated from him like rain clouds coalescing across a midnight sky. ''I specifically asked you not to—''

''Laura didn't mind.'' Although Alexa trembled inside at the sharp edge in his tone, she kept her voice breezy.

His eyes flashed rare annoyance. ''That's not the point. We agreed—''

''You think my grandparents could have hired Leo? He brought them all a picnic lunch.''

''You're trying to divert me by changing the subject.''

''We aren't going to agree on this one. Besides, I don't find it pleasant when you're angry with me,'' she admitted, hoping her words would make him realize that she did care about his wishes—even if she went against them.

Just then, Cameron's cell phone rang. ''Sorry, someone might need me.'' He flipped open the phone and listened for a moment, then snapped it shut. ''That was the sheriff.''

''And?'' There was something he didn't want to tell her. Something he was considering that he wanted to protect her from.

''Remember the references those security guards used in Denver?''

''Yes.''

''The phone bills were paid by money order.''

''So they can't be traced.''

''Probably not, but we did learn something interesting.''

"What?"

"You aren't going to like it."

"But I should know, right?"

"The phone bills were sent to a post-office box...
in Boston."

Chapter Twelve

At the raw pain in Cameron's voice, Alexa embraced him, her hands curling up his back, her chest, hips and thighs pressed to him. He gathered her close, breathing in her scent as she tipped her head back and looked into his eyes.

Alexa nibbled her bottom lip. "I don't understand what you're thinking. My grandparents live in Boston and Sandra died in Boston. But they had no reason to murder Sandra, since she didn't know about the trust fund."

The fact that she had accepted that the grandparents who had raised her could be capable of such a deed pained Cameron. He couldn't imagine how it must be for her to suspect her only living relatives of such ugliness.

"Exactly. But if those bills were sent to Boston, perhaps we've been looking in the wrong direction." Heat filled him, and deep inside, muscles tightened around a kindled ember. He ached to kiss her. He had trouble concentrating and dipped his head until his lips almost touched hers.

"Wait a minute. Sandra was mugged in the park.

You think it might have been premeditated? That whoever murdered Sandra caused the trouble here? What makes you think that?"

"The possibility hadn't occurred to me before now." His fingers traced slow, lazy circles at the base of her neck. He enjoyed his effect on her, enjoyed watching her pupils dilate and feeling her pulse quicken. Enjoyed watching her lose to the pull of desire.

She trembled at his caress. "Did you have any enemies in Boston?"

He drank in her response and ran his hands through her hair. "There are lots of crazy people in this world. Maybe some patient's relatives blamed me when their loved one died."

"That's crazy."

"Whoever let that bull loose, blew up the bridge and the stable isn't exactly what I'd call sane." She shivered against him, and he rubbed her arms to warm her, but he knew he wouldn't succeed. Despite her passionate nature, cold fear had taken over as she considered the possibilities.

She shivered again. "Don't forget the stalker didn't just attack us, he went after the twins. It's almost as if someone has a vendetta against your entire family."

Cam didn't want to think about his family right now. Nor did he want to think about danger and intrigue.

He often found a solution to a puzzle would pop into his mind if he relaxed. And he could think of no better way to take his mind off his problems than a little relaxation with Alexa.

"Come on, let's get you warm." He led her downstairs, past the fireplace to the hot tub off the pool. The hot tub had been designed deep and wide to hold four to six people. He was glad for the privacy fence, glad to have Alexa alone. He left the lights off, except for one pink underwater light that reflected through the water in enticing rays.

As the night air blew across the privacy fence, goose bumps rose on Alexa's flesh. "I thought you were going to make me warm?"

"Oh, I am—right after you take off your clothes," he teased as he started to strip. He couldn't wait to try out his new toy with Alexa. "Last one in has to…"

He jumped first into the hot tub without finishing his sentence. Letting the warm water swirl over his bare flesh didn't change his temperature much. His skin, already heated from thoughts of Alexa, adapted easily to the water.

Cameron rose to the surface and flicked on the whirlpool jets. He turned to watch Alexa slide into the water, her back arched, her breasts high and aroused in the pink water.

She tilted her head back on the ledge with a contented sigh. "This feels wonderful."

He shifted his body close to hers and claimed her lips in one possessive swoop, let the heat chase away the cold, let the soft light banish the shadows. She kissed him willingly, pulling him to her, her mouth fitting his perfectly, making the ache spread through his body until he needed her with a force that shook him.

Refusing to deny himself, he drank deeply from

her mouth, letting his tongue move over hers. Then he felt the liquid movement of her hips against his sex.

"Not yet." Ending the kiss caused him pain. Backing away cost him. But she was worth every bit of patience he could summon, worth the savage pleasure she gave him with her eagerness. Worth waiting to bury himself in her heat.

Without his body to block her, her toes floated to the surface, and he nipped the arch of her foot. His hands kneaded her feet as he ignored his aching arousal.

She giggled and tried to pull away, watching him with a breathless combination of wariness, excitement and pleasure. "That tickles."

Urgency roughened his tone but he kept himself under control. "Too bad. You have to hold still. You lost the bet."

"What bet?"

"You were the last one in, so you have to do whatever I ask for the next hour."

Her breath drew in sharply. "I never made any such bet." Her protest, lazy with indignation and a hint of curiosity, lacked conviction.

"Hold still," he demanded as his lips traced a path from her pearly pink toenails, past her delicate ankles to her parted knees.

"Oh."

"What's wrong?"

"The whirlpool…"

He swallowed a knowing grin and returned to exploring the tantalizing softness of her legs, the gleaming ripeness of her thighs. She had a terrific body, and her legs called to him, the smooth silky muscles quivering as he parted her legs wider and raised her hips to his mouth.

"Cameron—" Surprise and hunger made her tremble with anticipation.

"It's all right." He fully intended to taste all of her—and he would wait until she wanted him as much as he wanted her.

Cameron knew his patience would reward both of them. Although she wriggled and squirmed, he avoided the spot where they both desired his lips most. He tasted her thighs, her hips, the hollow at her waist as she floated in the water, open to him and content to let him have his way.

Only content wasn't quite the right word. Little moans of pleasure came from deep in her throat, a sound he could become quite accustomed to hearing. Holding back had never been so difficult. He wanted her badly. Wanted to thrust into her heat and feel those silky thighs around his waist, hear her purr turn to a shout of satisfaction.

But not yet.

Water glistened over her skin. Pink shimmers of water lapped at her flesh. She had no idea how much he wanted her.

But he waited, wanting to show her how good they were together, and he'd hold back until he'd done so—even if it killed him.

"Cameron?"

"Hmm?" She wasn't hot enough yet.

Slowly he maneuvered her parted legs over a jet, adjusting the pressure and direction of the spurting water until she tensed in pleasure.

"Relax, darling. We have all night."

She lifted her head, her eyes dilated with need, her voice urgent. "I can't…relax. I'm not sure I can wait one more second."

"But you'll wait for me, won't you? I want to be inside you when you explode. Tell me, you'll wait."

"I'll try."

"Not good enough." He eased her away from the water jet. "Promise me," he demanded softy.

"I promise. But you don't know how good I feel."

"Tell me." He floated her back over the jet.

"My skin is hot and hotter. It's hard to breathe. And my heart is beating too fast. And if I don't move, I'm going to die."

"Don't move, sweetheart. And remember your promise." Then his mouth came down over her and she tasted so sweet, he wondered how he'd ever recover if she left him. Her hips bucked and he supported her legs with his arms, pinning her open for him against the hot tub's wall.

She flailed and reached for his hair to tug his mouth away and drag him upward. Gently he replaced her hand on the pool's edge. "Patience."

"I'm…going…to get…even."

He breathed more sweet torment into her. "I can hardly wait."

But he couldn't wait. Not another second.

Breathing brokenly, he thrust into her and she welcomed him with a throaty whimper. Her breath rushed out, his name on her lips.

He paused to angle another jet onto her sweet flesh. And she arched upward.

"Wait. Wait, just a few more minutes," he coaxed.

He pumped back and forth slowly, enjoying the exquisite sensations of silky heat and burning nerve endings. And when he could hold back no more, he moved his hips faster.

She clutched his shoulders, frantic, her hips meeting his, matching him move for move, thrust for thrust. Giving herself to him completely, she shuddered against him, her nails raking his back as she dragged him with her into a fiery intimacy, rocking them both with a series of explosions that left him weak, breathless and very much in love.

ALEXA AWOKE in Cameron's bedroom. They'd made love several more times last night, leaving her satisfied and lazy and just a bit sore. She desperately wanted coffee and a shower, but Cameron's arm across her hip kept her pinned to the bed.

She moved his arm without waking him and wondered if he normally slept this deeply or if his exhaustion was due to his strenuous activities last night. Alexa hurried to the shower, wondering why she didn't smell breakfast being made. Had Leo slept in? She'd kill for a sip of caffeine but would settle for brushing her teeth, a hot shower, soothing body lotion and a quick manicure to make her feel human again.

After her long shower, Alexa returned to her room for a fresh set of clothes. Although the shower had revived her, she still wanted coffee and again wondered if Leo had slept in for she still didn't smell any food. Perhaps she'd try her hand in the kitchen and serve Cameron breakfast in bed.

Alexa eased open her bedroom door and stepped inside. Hundreds of big fat scorpions marched across the wall like an army of invading soldiers. With a shriek, Alexa backed into the hall and slammed her door.

She rammed into something hard and let out another yelp.

"Steady." Cameron's strong arms gripped her and she realized she'd bumped into him. He'd run naked into the hallway without taking a moment to pull on his pants. And his main concern was for her. "What's wrong?"

She forced her throat and mouth to work past her fright. "My room is full of scorpions." Turning, she hurried to the twins' room. "Let's make sure they're okay."

Cameron got there first and opened the door. The room was empty of scorpions and children, and he let out a sigh of relief. "Julie must have taken them for breakfast and a ride."

Alexa tried to control her shaking. If she had gone to her room last night, instead of Cameron's, she might not be alive right now. "Cam, there're too many scorpions in my room for them to have gotten there by themselves."

Cam gathered her into his arms and ushered her back to his room. Alexa dressed in yesterday's clothes with a grimace. Cam's silence grated on her nerves, but she knew him well enough by now to know his mind was busy sifting through possibilities and alternatives, and he would make a connection she couldn't in her frightened state. So she waited.

"This is the first attack on you alone. I always assumed you'd been in danger because you were with me or the twins. But it appears as if we are all in danger."

Alexa shivered. "You're supposed to be making me feel better, not worse. Our problems were supposed to be over after the custody hearing."

"Maybe we were wrong and the dangers had nothing to do with the hearing or your grandparents," Cam suggested.

"Maybe. Look, I just can't think without coffee. And I'd rather put a full flight of stairs between me and those scorpions." She glanced toward her room with a shudder and wondered if the deadly creatures could travel under the door.

Cameron put on jeans, a shirt and boots, then they both went down to the kitchen. There were no signs of Julie and the twins or Leo. The house was so quiet Alexa could have heard a tear dropping on the kitchen floor.

There were no dirty cereal bowls in the sink, not even a hint of the aroma of coffee or bacon. But then, both Julie and Leo kept the house spotless. Alexa opened the dishwasher, looking for signs of breakfast. The machine was empty, and panic replaced her feelings of unease.

"Let's go see if the ponies are still here."

Cameron looked up from the coffeemaker, his eyes dark with concern. "I thought you wanted coffee."

"Something's wrong. I don't think Julie and Leo

have been here." Alexa gestured at the dishwasher.
"There aren't any dirty dishes around."

"Leo could have washed the dishes and unloaded
it," Cam suggested, but he was already moving toward the back door. Ever since his old stable burned
down, they'd kept the children's ponies and Julie's
horse in a hay shed out back. Most of the other
horses were let loose in open pastures to graze on
the summer grasses until the stable could be rebuilt.

Alexa and Cam hurried to the shed. Cameron
shoved open the door and looked inside. "Julie's car
is here. So are three of the four kittens. Both ponies
and Julie's horse are gone. She must have taken them
for a ride."

Alexa frowned, unable to banish a niggle of worry.
"She didn't say anything to me about a ride."

"The twins may have talked her into it." Cam
pulled out his cell phone. "I'd feel better if she'd
left a note or we could check with Leo. Remind me
to buy Julie a cell phone."

"We're probably worrying for nothing. They'll
likely all come riding in within the hour," Alexa
agreed as she scanned the horizon for two little boys
and their sitter.

Cam dialed the phone, then ended the call without
speaking to anyone. "Leo's not home, either."

An hour later there was still no sign of Julie and
the boys, and Cam had alerted all the ranch hands to
be on the lookout. Four hours later they were positive
something was very wrong.

"Maybe they stopped for a picnic and the horses
ran off," Alexa suggested.

"Maybe."

Alexa admired Cam's calm, but she could see the worry in his eyes, hear the tension in his voice. He'd notified the sheriff, Tyler had mobilized a group of neighbors to help, and Rafe had gone up in the helicopter to do an overhead search. There was nothing left to do but wait.

The ranch was huge, a full four days ride from east to west and almost that from north to south. The land encompassed rivers and mountains and ravines and creeks. By early evening it was obvious that Julie would never have voluntarily kept the twins out so long. And where was Leo?

And as the sun fell behind the mountains, so did their hopes of finding the boys before morning. Alexa brought Cam a sandwich and coffee. He accepted the drink and ignored the food. All afternoon they'd searched the area where the boys and Julie usually rode and were finally forced to come in and rest their weary horses.

Alexa sat beside Cam on the front porch, knowing he burned to continue a night search—on foot if necessary, but knew it was foolhardy. "At least it's warm tonight."

"The Senator's bringing in more help tomorrow." Cam told her. "I just wish I could do something more. I feel so helpless."

The waiting was eating away at her. Alexa had filed her nails down to nubs, blistered her feet from pacing and had trouble controlling her tone to keep from snapping at everyone who was trying to help. Cody had cleaned out the scorpions in the bedroom, but she couldn't even consider sleeping with the twins still missing. Her place was here with Cameron.

"No one's found Leo in town. Do you think that's suspicious?"

"I don't know. Maybe he and Julie are together with the boys."

"Can you think of anywhere else Julie may have stopped?" Alexa asked. "Maybe a nearby cabin, a neighbor's, a cave?"

"She never rode out for more than an hour or two. The boys can't sit still in the saddle longer than that."

"Maybe Julie mentioned something to her roommate," Alexa suggested. "Why don't we ride into town and check? If we find nothing there, we should check with Leo's neighbors. Someone may know where to find him."

Cameron's voice wasn't argumentative or commanding or angry. It was as if the loss of the boys had created a dead icy spot inside him that made his eyes into gray pools of despair. "I'm not leaving."

She couldn't bear to see him in such misery. She knew better than to urge him to eat or sleep. How could he when she couldn't, either? "You have your cell phone. The sheriff and his men have taken over the kitchen. They'll call if there's news. Wouldn't you rather do something?" she coaxed.

JULIE LIVED in a dorm by the community college. Cam drove over without much hope of finding anything that would help. He knew Alexa was simply trying to keep him busy, but it made sense to cover all the bases.

Perhaps Julie had mentioned something useful to her roommate. Perhaps the roommate had noticed someone following Julie. Perhaps Julie had mentioned being frightened. Ever since she'd been attacked on the way back from the portable toilet, he'd felt responsible for her safety. But Leo had always been there as an unofficial guard.

And after the fiasco of hiring the security team, Cameron had preferred not to bring more strangers onto the ranch. Another mistake. Although the sheriff thought the twins and Julie might have run into trouble with the horses, Cam suspected their trouble was the human kind.

Tomorrow they would find them. Alexa had to be correct. It was warm, and the twins and Julie would survive the night—even without food and water. And Julie was no fool. She always packed boxes of juice and snacks for the boys in her saddlebags. They would be fine. Once they returned safe and sound, the twins would be talking about their adventure for months.

Alexa looked at Cam worriedly and knocked on the dorm door. Alexa had shadows under her eyes, her cheeks were hollow, and her lips raw from nervously biting her lips. She wanted the twins back every bit as much as he did, and that knowledge made him love her all the more.

Loud country music blocked out her knock. Cam pounded harder, and finally a young woman answered the door. She wore heavy eye makeup, and her hair was teased out around her head in a most unbecoming fashion.

Cam forced himself to smile pleasantly. "Can we talk to you about Julie?"

"Julie?"

"Julie Edwards. I'm afraid she and my boys may have met up with an accident. They're missing."

The woman let them inside the dorm and turned down the stereo. "You must be Cameron Sutton. I'm Patricia Truitt." She frowned at Cameron and Alexa. "How long has Julie been missing?"

"Since this morning," Cam explained.

Alexa looked around the cheap apartment. "When was the last time you saw her?"

Patricia glanced at the ceiling as if seeking an answer there. "Last week?"

Cam and Alexa exchanged puzzled looks. Before Cam could ask another question, Patricia volunteered Julie's whereabouts. "She's been staying with Leo Harley at his camper."

The sheriff had already checked Leo's address. He was gone, too. Cam's stomach started to churn. If Julie and the twins had just had a mishap while out riding, then Leo's being missing didn't make sense. But if Julie and Leo had taken off somewhere with the twins...

Cam could hardly believe he was thinking that Leo had betrayed him. Julie had vouched for him and he and Sandra had always thought of Julie as part of the family. He suddenly recalled that Julie had been in Boston when Sandra had been killed. Julie could have sent the telephone bills for the fake security guard's reference to a Boston post-office box. And Julie could have faked her own attack to gain their trust and allay their suspicions.

But although she'd had the means and opportunity to commit the crimes, she didn't have a motive. Nor did Leo have a motive, unless he was trying to force Julie to do something against her will by threatening the kids.

"Would you mind if we looked around her room?" Alexa asked.

"I don't know." Patricia hesitated. "Julie doesn't like anyone to go in there."

"We won't touch anything," Alexa promised.

Patricia walked over to an ashtray and plucked out a key. "I guess she won't have to know."

"We won't tell her." Cam tried not to get his hopes up as he opened the door and flicked on the light.

Beside him, Alexa drew in a breath. Horror tingled down Cam's spine at the sight of the wall by Julie's bed. His baby-sitter was insane. She had pictures of Cam and Sandra—with Sandra's face cut out and a picture of Julie's face replacing it. Julie had thrown darts at a picture of Alexa and Cameron taken at the wedding.

And now he knew Julie's motive. She had a sick crush on him.

Over her dresser, she'd blown up a poster of Cameron's face, tacked one of his old shirts under it and attached a pair of his jeans he'd forgotten he'd lost. On the ceiling were pictures and stories about the twins and the Levenger legacy that made his sons two of the richest little boys in the world.

Her voice shaky, Alexa grabbed his arm. "Don't touch anything."

Shaken and more worried than ever about his sons, Cam took out his cell phone. "I'm calling the FBI."

IT TOOK MOST of the night for the FBI, the sheriff and Cameron to put the pieces of the puzzle together. Back at Cameron's house they went over the facts.

Leo Harvey was Julie Edwards's friend. He wasn't too bright, but he'd had a crush on Julie and would do whatever she asked. He'd been dishonorably discharged from the military special forces after he'd failed to take enough care during his training on explosives.

The information about Julie made Cameron shake with anger and frustration. She had grown up in a series of foster homes and been sponsored by Judge Stewart, who'd recommended her to the Suttons as a baby-sitter. Unfortunately the judge had believed that Julie's troubles with the law during her teenage years were long over, and he'd sealed her files.

Her college entrance exams showed Julie to have an exceptionally high IQ. Personality profiles showed her stable. But once the court ordered documents were revealed, several disturbing facts came to light.

Cam and Alexa read the file with the FBI over a pot of coffee in his living room. When Julie was fifteen her foster mother died under mysterious circumstances, and her foster father claimed Julie had made sexual advances on him. Julie claimed *he* made the advances, and in court Judge Stewart believed her.

Cam wondered if this was the second time she'd gotten away with murder after developing a crush on a man. That he had trusted her made him ill. That she had taken his sons made him frantic.

He tossed the file onto the table. "It still doesn't make sense."

Alexa squeezed Cameron's hand. "She may have killed Sandra, thinking you'd turn to her. When you didn't, she decided to try and get rid of me."

Cam thought about the explosions at the stable and on the bridge. "And when that didn't work, she became so enraged she tried to kill us both?"

"Maybe." Alexa sighed. "You may not ever have been her target. Leo bungled the explosives. They may just have gone off at the wrong time. It was *me* she wanted to scare off, and when that didn't work, she wanted me dead—so she could have you."

"And now she's taken the boys. But why?" Cam dropped his head into his hands. She could be anywhere by now, and the twins could be terrified...or worse.

Alexa tugged Cam to his feet. "Come on. You need a walk to clear your head."

He followed her onto the porch. "Why did she take the twins?"

"I don't think she'll hurt them. She loves those boys."

Cam knew that Alexa was trying to look on the bright side, but it wasn't helping. "She loved me, too, in her sick way, but that didn't stop her from almost killing me. I was an idiot to trust her. What kind of doctor am I that I couldn't see she had problems?"

"You aren't a shrink. And beating yourself up won't bring the boys back." Alexa pulled him down the drive as if compelled to keep moving. "No one suspected her. None of us."

"She was right here in the house almost all the time. She seemed so innocent."

"Where would she take the twins?"

Alexa was thinking more clearly than he was. The past couldn't be changed. He had to let go of his mistake, concentrate on getting the twins back.

Cam's cell phone rang. He answered it listlessly. "Hello."

At the sound of Julie's voice, Cam held the phone so both he and Alexa could hear. "If you want to see the boys alive, bring one million dollars in un-marked bills to the Bird's Nest at noon tomorrow. Bring Alexa. If we see the law, your brothers or any-one but you and Alexa, you'll never see the twins again."

Cam's heart pounded. "How do I know the boys are still alive?"

"Hi, Daddy." Jason's voice came over the phone and Cam's heart clutched.

"I'll see you soon," Cam promised.

"I miss you," Flynn said, and Cam knew he was crying. The boys sensed something was wrong. He'd never let them go away overnight before—not even with Julie.

"I miss you, too."

The phone clicked before Cam even finished his sentence. He looked at Alexa and knew he couldn't risk going back inside to the FBI. She wasn't a good liar, and hope was written all over her face.

"Oh, God." Alexa gripped his hand, her nails dig-ging into his flesh. "Where's the Bird's Nest?"

"It's an old silver mine in the mountains."

Alexa frowned. "I can have my bank wire the funds. But can we get that much money changed into cash by noon?"

Chapter Thirteen

It turned out that dipping into Alexa's trust fund wasn't necessary, but Cameron appreciated her unselfish offer. The Senator kept a safe on the ranch's premises, with cash for emergencies. Between that and Cameron's withdrawal from the bank, they'd come up with the funds necessary to ransom the twins.

Cameron worried about the twins, hoping they weren't terrified. Julie's voice had sounded so tense and wild he couldn't be sure she wouldn't hurt them.

And he also worried about Julie's request for Alexa to accompany him. If Julie wanted just money, there was no need for her to specify that Alexa should be there to make the exchange. So he didn't say a word of protest when Rafe slipped Alexa a semiautomatic pistol.

In all likelihood, if anyone checked them for weapons, they'd only check Cameron. And if the weapon made Alexa feel more protected, he wanted her to have it. He knew her well enough to realize she wouldn't have accepted the gun if she didn't know how to use it. No doubt her exclusive European finishing school had taught marksmanship, as well as riding.

As partners went, he had every confidence in Alexa. She might be a bundle of simmering passion hidden by cultured poise, but in a pinch, she could think straight. And with the way his nerves jittered, he wanted all the calm around him he could get.

"How much farther?" Alexa asked. She pulled up, took a swig from her water bottle and tipped back her hat to look at him.

As usual, every hair was in place. Her lipstick and makeup were perfect. She'd even used makeup to hide the dark circles he knew were under her eyes.

Cam took his bearings from the ranch below and the mountains above. They rode a narrow trail toward the rugged high country. With trails this steep, they had to use cutbacks and couldn't go in a straight line. "Several more hours."

To her credit, Alexa bit back a groan. Instead, she glanced at her watch. "We better get moving."

"You think I'm making a mistake, don't you?"

"By not calling in the law or your brothers?" Alexa shrugged. "It's your call, Cameron. They're your boys."

She'd said "your boys," not "our boys," and that bothered Cam almost as much as second-guessing Julie's intentions. The more he knew of Alexa, the more he saw in her to love. She had a sassy way about her, but wasn't too pushy. She had sense when it counted, and her prim attitude disappeared when he removed her clothes.

And she adored the twins. She might spend his money with a heavy hand, but she hadn't thought twice about offering *her* money to save the boys. Complex, confident and interesting, she may not have been the right woman for him, but nonetheless, she'd stolen his heart.

She rode beside him without complaining, although he knew she had to be sore. Back straight, eyes bright and curious, she looked eager to meet up with Julie Edwards.

"What's the plan?" Alexa asked him.

Cameron shrugged. "We give Julie the money. She gives us the twins."

"I want to see the twins first."

Cameron shook his head. "Julie holds all the cards. I won't put my sons in danger."

"And she has no reason to give them to us, unless you demand to see the boys first."

Cameron nodded. Alexa had a point. He might not care about the money, but he wanted to keep his boys safe. If that required playing the hard-ass, he could do it. All he had to do was recall his boys' last words to him, and anger fired through him. How dare Julie put his sons through such an ordeal? There could be long-term emotional consequences. Nightmares. Pain.

Damn her. Why hadn't he noticed Julie's attraction to him? She'd held on to him too tightly after he carried her from the portable toilet, but he'd thought it was fear that made her clutch so. And at his wedding when she'd burst into tears, he should have seen that her tears weren't of joy, but heartbreak.

He'd been too involved with Alexa to notice or think about Julie Edwards—especially since he'd never had a romantic thought about her. He'd never encouraged her craziness. Another woman would have gotten over her crush and moved on.

He clenched and unclenched his fist as he led his horse around a hummock. Up ahead the trail leveled off for a mile or two before it climbed again toward the mine. He forced thoughts of the past away and surveyed his surroundings. Even up this high, the mountain grasses were green, the forest lush. A stream, an offshoot of a waterfall, trickled nearby, and he saw a white-tailed deer pause to drink from the stream. Startled by the deer, a rabbit scooted for cover. A blue jay took flight. It was hard to believe that in all this peace, his children were in danger. He would never forgive Julie for frightening his babies.

Stop it.

He needed to keep his wits about him. Enough about revenge and could-have-dones and should-have-seens. Berating himself wouldn't help the twins.

He smelled smoke long before they rounded the final bend and saw smoke curling from the mine entrance. Eager, he pushed forward. He wanted the exchange over with and the boys back in his arms.

"Hold it right there, Doc." Leo Harley stepped out of the trees, a rifle aimed at Cameron's chest.

Cameron eased his mount to a halt. "Whatever you say. I just want the twins back."

Leo ignored Alexa. "Climb down, Doc. I need to make sure you aren't armed."

Cameron held his arms wide and tried to appear harmless. "I don't have a weapon."

"Let's make sure, Doc." Leo came forward and frisked Cameron efficiently. Then he motioned them toward the cabin. "You can walk the rest of the way."

Alexa dismounted and started to loop the horses' reins to a low-hanging tree branch.

Leo shook his massive head. "Bring the horses."

Alexa did as he ordered. "What do you want me for?"

Leo shrugged. "Julie's orders."

"You take orders from a woman?" Alexa asked in an attempt to drive a small wedge between the accomplices.

Leo snarled, and fear and pride lit his tone. "Julie always gets what she wants. Anyone who stands in her way gets hurt."

Cameron didn't make any threatening moves and did as Leo asked. "Are the twins hurt?"

"Naw." Leo shook his head. "She keeps the brats sleeping so they won't be any trouble."

Alarm zapped through Cameron. Although sleeping boys couldn't be frightened, the danger of overdosing two-year-olds was very real. Judging medication for children was done by weight, but it wasn't an exact science. A little too much could cause brain damage, lead to a coma—even death.

He'd brought his medical bag with his bedroll, but out here in the wilderness, he could do very little. He consoled himself with the knowledge that Rafe was standing by with the helicopter. A quick call from the radio or cell phone would bring his brother flying in within minutes.

As they walked up to the mine entrance, Leo eyed Cam's bulging saddlebags greedily. "You brought all the money?"

Remembering Alexa's concerns, Cam kept his voice reasonable but firm. "You can count it *after* I see that the twins are safe."

Leo pushed him forward with the gun. "That's not Julie's plan."

Cameron held his ground. "I don't give a rat's ass about Julie. Can't you see that she's using you?"

Pointing a gun at Alexa, Julie stepped out of the mine, her face angry, her cheeks wet with tears. "You never did care about me, Cam. I took care of your children and you never even thanked me for all I did for you."

At the wild look in Julie's eyes, Cam damned himself for his careless words. He'd let anger and fear do his talking, and he had to try to repair the damage. Try to start a fight between Leo and Julie. He chose his next words—an outright lie—to the unstable Julie with extreme care. "I thought you loved Leo."

Julie wiped away her tears, but her gun stayed pointed at Alexa. The college student's voice rose an octave, almost to a screech. "You thought wrong."

Leo's meaty lips turned down. "But you said—"

"I said what I needed to say to get you to help me," Julie boasted. "And I don't want to hear any complaints out of you. We're going to be rich, Leo. Now—" she faced Cameron "—bring me the money."

"First we want to see the twins," Alexa insisted.

Leo started toward the mine.

"Forget it. I give the orders." Julie held up her hand, stopping Leo. Her voice turned eerily calm. "No way is she taking *my* babies and *my* man. Kill her, Leo."

Leo looked from Julie to Cameron, his face red with rage. Eyes lit like a fuse, lips twisted with humiliation, he looked ready to explode.

Cameron waited, balancing on the balls of his feet, bunching his muscles, ready to attack.

Leo had finally figured out that Julie had used him. Julie didn't love him. And the knowledge boiled into fury.

Cameron watched Leo's eyes fill with hatred. Then Leo raised his gun, pointed it at Alexa, tightened his finger on the trigger.

Cameron shoved Alexa aside and lunged for Leo's weapon, knocking Leo's wrist into the air. A bullet whizzed by his head, and then the two men rolled onto the grass, pummeling each other with their free hands.

Cameron focused on the hand holding Leo's gun. He took a blow to his chin, but he didn't release pressure on Leo's wrist. His knowledge of anatomy came in handy. Leo's wrists might be massive, but the bones could only take so much pressure.

At the sickening snap, Leo roared like a bull, slamming his forehead down. Cameron ducked at the last second, avoiding a broken nose. He brought his knee up, hard. Straight into Leo's groin. Leo twisted, and Cam's blow glanced ineffectively off Leo's massive thigh.

Somewhere Leo found a rock. He raised it over Cam's head, ready to strike a killing blow.

Several gunshots sounded, and simultaneously, a huge red spot stained Leo's shirt. The rock dropped harmlessly to his side and he keeled over, unconscious.

On shaky legs, Cameron stood and took his bearings. Alexa lay on the ground, the gun she'd shot Leo with resting on her thigh. She motioned with the gun for him to go. "Julie's getting away with the twins. Go."

Cam heard Jason and Flynn cry out sleepily from the mine. He paused halfway between his sons and Alexa. Alexa looked a little pale, but then, she'd just shot a man. Torn between helping Alexa to her feet and going to the twins, he hesitated. "Are you okay?"

"I'm fine. Get the boys."

Figuring Leo was no longer a danger to Alexa, Cameron scooped up Leo's gun and followed Julie into the mine. He burst inside, and his eyes took a moment to adjust to the darkness. Empty tin cans of food, candy-bar wrappers and sleeping bags littered the floor.

A cot stood in the corner. It was empty.

But Cam had explored the mine with his brothers when they were boys and knew there was a second entrance, just off the main artery. He hurried inside and rounded the bend, then raced outside again, sure that Julie had taken the boys out the mine's side entrance. Cameron suspected she'd hidden a four-wheel-drive vehicle there for her escape.

Fear for his sons' safety urged his feet faster. He raced after Julie and skidded around the bend and back out into open air.

Sure enough, she was lifting the sleepy twins into the back seat of a Jeep. Cam's relief that the boys were semiconscious tempered his fury.

He reminded himself Julie was unbalanced—just

as she spun around and aimed her gun at him. His fist connected with her wrist and threw off her aim as she pulled the trigger. The bullet spit by harmlessly.

In pain from the force of his block on her arm, she dropped the gun.

Rage and tears combined, she attacked him with her hands. "You should have loved me. *Me*. Not Sandra. Not Alexa. *Me!*"

Her raving made her violent, dangerous and unpredictable. Cam had never struck a woman in his life, couldn't bring himself to do so now. He shifted to the side and swept her feet out from under her. She fell hard and he scooped up her gun, placed it in the waistband of his jeans.

"We could still make it work," she pleaded with him, proving once again how unbalanced she was.

He checked his boys' pulses and kept a wary eye on Julie. "You murdered Sandra, didn't you?"

Julie raised her chin. "I did it for us. So you could inherit her money and we could be together."

"I didn't care about Sandra's money. I loved her."

"And I killed Alexa, so now you are free."

"What?" Cam's heart stopped and skipped several beats. Alexa was fine. She'd told him she was fine.

Julie smoothed back her hair, oblivious to his confusion. "You're free to marry me. She's dead. Or she soon will be. I shot her in the gut. After all the trouble she caused me, she deserves a slow and painful death."

Horror stabbed him, made his hands shake. He took the keys from the Jeep's ignition and slipped them into his pocket. He picked up Flynn, then Jason, and hurried back to Alexa. Julie wouldn't get far on foot.

He suddenly recalled Alexa's pallor and weak voice, which he'd attributed to her having shot Leo. He hadn't seen any blood, but then, she'd twisted away, so he hadn't gotten a good view.

Cameron needed to call Rafe and the chopper, but he didn't have a free hand. It seemed to take him forever to reach Alexa. He gently placed the sleepy boys on the ground beside her and reached for the cell phone.

He turned her over and paled at the wound. There was blood. Too much blood. He tried to staunch the bleeding while he called Rafe on his cell phone.

The helicopter ride was a nightmare. At least the boys slept through it. Cameron knew Alexa wouldn't make it to the hospital without a transfusion. Luckily he matched Alexa's A positive. He started giving her his blood until he barely remained conscious.

Then he slumped, vowing that whatever happened, if Alexa lived, he wouldn't pressure her to stay. She'd practically given her life to save the twins. It would be selfish of him to ask more of her.

He loved her so much. He loved her enough to let her go. But first—she had to live.

ALEXA OPENED HER EYES, and the first thing she saw was Cameron. ''You look terrible.'' Her voice came out in a croak, and she licked her dry lips and looked around the room.

A bright light glared at her. Machines beeped, and she figured out she was in a hospital bed.

Chin dark with stubble, eyes darker with worry, Cam leaned over her. "Don't try to move. You're hooked up to a few monitors and an IV's in your wrist."

She felt his hand holding hers and squeezed. "Love you."

"Sounds good, but I won't hold you responsible. You're on heavy-duty drugs. But you're going to make it."

She recalled rising out of her body, a long tunnel filled with light. And Sandra hugging her. "Sandra told me it wasn't my time. She sent me back. And I do love you."

His brow rose skeptically. "Uh-huh."

She could tell he thought she wasn't lucid, but she'd never been so sure of anything in her life. As she'd lain on the ground, her life's blood leaking out of her, all she could think about was Cameron and the twins. Not some precious job that took her all over of the world. Not unearthing a piece of art from some dusty attic. Not pocketing a finder's fee.

She wanted Cameron. She wanted the twins. She wanted her family.

She wanted to tell Cam, but she couldn't find the strength. Her mouth was dry, her throat parched. He seemed to realize her need and lifted a glass with a straw to her mouth. Two small sips wasted her. The effort sent her to sleep.

When she awoke again, she felt stronger. A nurse hovered over her bed, checking the IV in her wrist. "How do you feel?"

"Like I've been shot."

"Are you in pain?"

"Not if you're going to put me back to sleep again." Alexa turned her head and took in the flowers spilling over from the nightstand and the dresser to the floor. The room smelled like heaven, and she breathed in deeply. A mistake. Breathing hurt.

"If you're up to it, you have visitors. But the doctor says they can only stay five—"

Cam strode into the room and glared at the nurse. "She's awake and you didn't tell me?"

"Where's my hairbrush?" Alexa asked, knowing she must look a wreck.

Cameron laughed and then he danced the frowning nurse around the room. "Now I know she's going to be all right."

At the commotion Chase and Laura stepped into the room. Laura ignored the dancing, crossed to the bed and gently used her own brush on Alexa's hair. Laura pulled out a small pink bottle and held it up. "I brought nail polish."

"Good. Maybe once I look more like myself, the big oaf will believe that I love him enough to stay in Colorado."

Cameron stopped dancing with the nurse who left the room. "I thought that was the morphine talking."

Laura handed Alexa the hairbrush and nail polish and tugged on Chase's arm. "We should leave."

Chase resisted her tug. "This is just getting interesting."

Cam shoved his brother toward the door. "Get out."

"I want to hear this," Chase protested.

"Hear what?" Rafe had apparently heard the commotion and entered the room, curious to know what was going on.

"Is anyone else listening outside?" Alexa asked, barely containing her grin. Grinning hurt. Yet with all the love shining out of Cameron's eyes, the concern in Laura's, the humor in Chase's and Rafe's, she figured that the Senator and Tyler couldn't be far behind.

Sure enough, the Senator and Tyler crowded into the room, each of them holding a twin. Keith ran to his father, and Chase lifted him into his arms. The only one missing was Laura and Chase's newest baby, and only because he was too young to expose to hospital germs.

"Okay, we're all here now," Rafe teased. "What's so important?"

"First," Alexa demanded, "someone tell me what happened to Julie and Leo."

"Leo's recovering while incarcerated in the county lockup," Cam told her. "Julie's in a Denver psychiatric hospital. She'll probably be judged unfit to stand trial."

"What's *incarpatrated?*" Flynn asked.

"What's a *sytrick?*"

No one answered the boys, and Alexa grinned, wondering how long the adult vocabulary could continue to keep the twins in the dark. Alexa helped change the subject. "So how did I get to the hospital?"

"Rafe flew you."

"Then I donated blood," Rafe bragged.

"Really?" Alexa looked to Cam for an explanation.

"You needed more blood after we landed at the hospital and I'd already given you what I could. So Rafe volunteered."

"What did we do in the helicopter, Uncle Rafe?" Jason asked, his tiny face screwed up into a frown. "I can't remember."

Rafe ruffled his hair. "You were blessedly quiet and followed my directions to sleep."

Flynn scratched his head. "And that helped?"

"We got Alexa to the hospital, didn't we?"

Alexa motioned for the twins to come closer and took their hands in hers. "Thanks for the help." Clearly they didn't remember much—if anything—of the entire incident, and she was relieved. They were bright enough to figure it out from all the talk, but they wouldn't remember being separated from their father, wouldn't remember their fears.

Rafe slapped Cam on the shoulder and looked at Alexa. "Now what made Cam so happy he was dancing with a nurse?"

"This is private," Cam growled.

"We're all family here," Chase said innocently.

"I love him and I'm staying," Alexa told them, knowing the words felt right.

Laura and Chase exchanged knowing grins. Tyler looked at his feet. Rafe chuckled. "Now that she's half-full of Sutton blood, she can't think straight."

"It must be the morphine," Tyler added, getting into the spirit of teasing Cameron.

The warmth and love surrounding her was incomparable to any feeling Alexa had ever known. She belonged with this man, with this family. She knew it in her heart and she knew it in her soul. "It's not the morphine. I know what I'm saying. I love him."

At her repeated announcement, Flynn and Jason exchanged high fives.

Rafe rolled his eyes. "Is that all?"

Tyler dug his elbow into Rafe. "Shh. Don't interrupt."

Alexa saw Laura wipe a stray tear from her eye. But Alexa was focused on Cameron.

Cameron leaned over her. "You don't have to leave your job. You can—"

"I won't be a part-time wife or part-time mother. I'm not ever going back to my job."

Cameron protested halfheartedly, probably to test her. "But you love your work."

"I've been thinking about opening a gallery in Highview." She winked at him, "It'll be expensive."

"Better hide your credit card," Chase warned.

"—But I'm staying here with you and the twins."

"For good?" Flynn asked.

"Forever?" Jason echoed.

"For as long as your dad wants me," Alexa agreed.

Flynn whispered to Jason, "Dad's smart."

Jason whispered to Flynn, "He won't ever let her go."

"That means we have a mother," Flynn told Jason, his voice full of awe.

"And we'll get more hugs and kisses and chocolate-chip cookies?" Flynn's voice rose on a hopeful note.

Without needing adult confirmation, the twins exchanged high fives again, big smiles and round eyes making them look, for once, more innocent than mischievous.

The nurse returned with another frown. "It's been more than five minutes. Everyone must leave."

"Good." Cam kissed Alexa gently on the mouth. "Everyone can leave except her doctor."

"Is that so?" The nurse raised an eyebrow.

"Yes, Nurse." Cameron leaned over Alexa protectively. "This doctor's going to keep kissing his wife until she's all better."

* * * * *

Don't miss the exciting conclusion of

THE SUTTON BABIES,
LULLABY AND GOODNIGHT

by Susan Kearney
Coming next month from
Harlequin Intrigue.

Turn the page for a sneak preview...

Chapter One

In Rhianna McCloud's hands rested the fate of her unborn child. The power to save and protect. Or the power to make a deadly mistake.

She vowed not to panic as she once again checked her trucks' rearview mirror. Rhianna swung a left turn toward Denver, hoping city streets and eyewitnesses might deter her pursuer. She prayed that her leaky radiator would hold out, that her rear tire wouldn't go flat again, that she wouldn't take a wrong turn and end up trapped and isolated on a country road. Or run out of gas.

The white sedan in relentless pursuit remained at a distance, never moving close enough for Rhianna to see the driver or make out the license plate. She had no idea who was driving that car. No idea who had broken into her place and gone through her belongings. But the invasion of her privacy had to end. The stalking had to end.

Jumpy nerves couldn't be good for the baby. She took one hand off the steering wheel and gently massaged her swollen stomach. Two more weeks. Two more weeks until her due date. The baby kicked, and the familiar thump reassured Rhianna. She had to be strong for her baby. Rafe Sutton's baby.

Replacing her hand on the wheel, she ignored the fear shimmying down her spine and the tightness of the seat belt against her stomach. She resisted the urge to slam the pedal to the metal. Her old pickup wasn't up for a road race, and her reflexes weren't as good as before her pregnancy.

She wished she had a cell phone or at least a CB radio to call for help, but those were luxuries this single mother-to-be couldn't afford. But her brain still worked, revving into overdrive at the danger.

While her truck sucked gas with an appetite as insatiable as a pregnant woman's was for peculiar foods, she believed she could make another three miles.

Rhianna caught a red light. Wished she had time to check her map. She didn't drive into Denver often, preferring the clean air of the mountains, the slower pace in the country and the companionship of friends and neighbors she'd known for years.

Rhianna turned right, and at the sight of the police station, she let out a relieved sigh. "It's okay, baby, we're going to make it."

But she'd spoken too soon. Her truck gurgled once and died. Desperate, Rhianna tried to restart the engine. But the gas gauge read empty.

One glance in the rearview mirror again and her heart rate doubled. The white sedan had pulled over behind her. Sun glinted off the window, and she still couldn't see her pursuer.

Eight and a half months pregnant she might be,

but Rhianna refused to sit like a rabbit snared in a trap. Releasing her seat belt, she opened the truck door.

And prepared to run for her life!

THE SECRET IS OUT!

HARLEQUIN®

I N T R I G U E®

presents

TEXAS CONFIDENTIAL

By day these agents are cowboys;
by night they are specialized
government operatives.
Men bound by love, loyalty and the law—
they've vowed to keep their missions
and identities confidential....

Harlequin Intrigue

Harlequin American Romance
(a special tie-in story)

HARLEQUIN®
Makes any time special ™

Visit us at www.eHarlequin.com

HITC

CELEBRATE VALENTINE'S DAY WITH HARLEQUIN®'S LATEST TITLE— *Stolen Memories*

Available in trade-size format, this collector's edition contains three full-length novels by *New York Times* bestselling authors Jayne Ann Krentz and Tess Gerritsen, along with national bestselling author Stella Cameron.

TEST OF TIME by Jayne Ann Krentz—
He married for the best reason.... She married for the only reason.... Did they stand a chance at making the only reason the real reason to share a lifetime?

THIEF OF HEARTS by Tess Gerritsen—
Their distrust of each other was only as strong as their desire. And Jordan began to fear that Diana was more than just a thief of hearts.

MOONTIDE by Stella Cameron—
For Andrew, Greer's return is a miracle. It had broken his heart to let her go. Now fate has brought them back together. And he won't lose her again...

Make this Valentine's Day one to remember!

Look for this exciting collector's edition on sale January 2001 at your favorite retail outlet.

HARLEQUIN®
® *Makes any time special* ™

Visit us at www.eHarlequin.com   PHSM

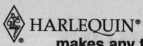
HARLEQUIN®
makes any time special—online...

eHARLEQUIN.com

shop eHarlequin

♥ Find all the new Harlequin releases at everyday great discounts.

♥ Try before you buy! Read an excerpt from the latest Harlequin novels.

♥ Write an online review and share your thoughts with others.

reading room

♥ Read our Internet exclusive daily and weekly online serials, or vote in our interactive novel.

♥ Talk to other readers about your favorite novels in our Reading Groups.

♥ Take our Choose-a-Book quiz to find the series that matches you!

authors' alcove

♥ Find out interesting tidbits and details about your favorite authors' lives, interests and writing habits.

♥ Ever dreamed of being an author? Enter our Writing Round Robin. The Winning Chapter will be published online! Or review our guidelines for submitting your novel.